I0659449

The Killing Road

A novel inspired by true events

By Scott Fields

Outer Banks Publishing Group
Raleigh/Outer Banks

The Killing Road. Copyright © 2016 by Scott Fields. All rights reserved. Published in the United States of America by Outer Banks Publishing Group – Outer Banks/Raleigh.

www.outerbankspublishing.com

No part of this book may be reproduced in any manner whatsoever without written permission except in the case of brief quotations embodied in critical articles and reviews. For information contact Outer Banks Publishing Group at

info@outerbankspublishing.com

All of the characters and events in this book are real, and any resemblance to actual events or actual persons living or dead, is intentional. Some events are fictional due to the literary dramatization of the story.

The names of the actual people involved have been changed at the request of the families.

Other works by Scott Fields

The Mansfield Killings

It was the worse two-week killing spree in Ohio's history. On the night of July 21, 1948, Robert Daniels and John West entered John and Nolena Niebel's house and forced the family into their car and drove them to a cornfield just off Fleming Falls Road in Mansfield.

Robert Daniels then shot each of them in the head. The brutal murders caught national attention in the media, but the killing spree didn't stop there. Three more innocent people would lose their lives at the hands of Daniels and West in the coming week.

Scott Fields tirelessly researched the killings, the capture and trial of Daniels and even interviewed a surviving member of the Niebel family to weave this tragic story into a must-read novel bringing the reader back to those dark days in the summer of 1948. It has been more than sixty years since the tragedy, and, yet, the why of it all still remains unanswered.

The killing spree is not only remembered to this day, but is an important and dark part of Mansfield lore.

Breakfast at the Diner

It has been two years since the death of his wife, and Frank Watson still struggles with the loss. Every morning, he meets with his friends at the local diner to talk and to exchange gossip, but inevitably must return to his farm that remains undisturbed since his wife's death.

Then, Pepper Ledley breezed into his life and a steamy romance begins. She was the new waitress in town nearly half his age and offered Frank something he had never before considered, a new beginning.

However, it somehow didn't seem right to Frank. How could he have these feelings when he still loved Ida? As he struggles with his new feelings and the memory of his beloved wife, Frank faces the biggest crisis of his life.

A large foreign corporation needs five hundred acres of land to build an egg factory and Frank alienates himself from the rest of the town when he, steadfastly, refuses to sell. What transpires is a web of deceit, manipulation and murder.

A Killing in a Small Town

Harlan Steelman owned most of the town of Bear Creek and found his way in and out of every backroom, barroom, and bedroom.

When his rival from high school, John Watson, returns to Bear Creek with his wife and son to start anew, Harlan vows to ruin John's life and take Kara, his wife, away from him.

When Harlan is found murdered, John Watson is the likely suspect and is taken into custody.

What happens next is the trial of the century for the little town of Bear Creek, but it takes a horrible twist at the end.

Summer Heat

If you read *Fifty Shades of Grey*, you'll like *Summer Heat*! When she was 17, there wasn't a man alive she would let get near her, and when she was 18, there wasn't a man she would keep away.

Women universally hated her, men continued to hold doors for her long after she passed by - just to watch her walk away.

Ninety-nine point nine percent of the men in Steam Corners wanted her, but she only wanted one man, Spencer Deacon. The one thing that Spencer didn't want was Jessie, and his firm and undeniable rejections infuriated her.

What followed was a series of sordid events involving murder, deceit, betrayal and the conviction of an innocent man.

All books are available on Amazon in print and as ebooks as well as available from Barnes & Noble and fine bookstores everywhere.

One

It was a small jail cell with a cot, a toilet, and a magazine that was over three years old. Dale opened his eyes and stared at the blood-stained wall. For a brief moment, he wondered what had happened to some poor inmate. He probably made the mistake of complaining about something and ended up paying the price. He rolled out of bed and placed his bare feet onto the cold floor. For some reason, the cold felt good to him. His head ached from the two bottles of gin he had drunk the night before. Dale ran his stained fingers throw his greasy hair.

"How in the hell did I get here?" he muttered.

There were those who described Dale Marlowe as having the eyes of the devil, and if you had seen him face-to-face, you would have said it too. He was a big man standing over six feet tall and weighed two hundred and twenty pounds. He glared at people with a cold, expressionless stare and had a personality that was nearly as threatening. Few people understood him, and even fewer wanted to.

A door opened, and a man dressed in a marshal's uniform stepped inside. He stopped and stared at Dale who was bent over holding his head with both hands.

"Man, you got a problem," he said still staring at Dale.

Dale said nothing. He didn't move.

"I'm going to let you go, but you need to think about getting some help. I've never seen anyone as drunk as you were last night."

Dale leaned back and slowly got to his feet.

"I'm letting you go, but I'm asking you to get out of this town," said the marshal. "We don't need the likes of you around here."

He led Dale out of the jail cell and into the main office. Dale started for the front door when the marshal handed him his wallet and keys. "Here's your belongings, now go find your car and get out of here."

Dale stumbled out the door and started to walk down the sidewalk. He remembered driving into the town and spending the evening in a bar, but he could not remember where he had parked his car. He continued walking down the street hoping to find it. It was his guess that it was probably parked in front of a bar.

Dale was born the month of July in 1946 in a small town in Wyoming. His father left when he was a young boy. He was gone most of the time so Dale never got to know him that well. The only information he was ever given about his father was from the horrid stories told by his mother. He took them in stride figuring they most likely were exaggerated to a certain degree. His mother worked two jobs leaving him alone most of his childhood. He never really knew what it was like having a mother and a father. There were those who claimed that being alone as a child was the reason he turned out the way he did. No one knew for sure; no one really cared.

Dale never finished school. He left home when he was seventeen roaming from town-to-town with no purpose in mind. He would settle in a town for a few days, find a job and would soon be fired for drinking or not showing up for work. His mother missed him, but was more than confident that someday she would read about him in the local newspaper, and it would tell how he was arrested for some illegal act or that he was killed while committing a crime.

As he had predicted, Dale found his car parked in front of Joe's Tavern. He grabbed the handle on the car door, paused and turned to the sign above the door. "Wonder if they're open," he muttered. He released the handle and walked over to the bar.

It was nearly pitch dark inside the tavern. The only source of light came from one dimly lit bulb and a few lighted beer signs. An older man stood behind the bar wiping the inside of a drinking glass with a towel. Four other men sat at the bar drinking beer. Dale started across the room and bumped into a table that was completely hidden by the darkness. He felt around until he found one of the chairs and sat down. He glanced over at the bar and found everyone including the owner was staring at him.

The owner sat down the glass and picked up another one. "We ain't open," he said.

"How come they're drinking then?" Dale asked.

"They're friends of mine, and you ain't."

"Then, how can I become a friend?"

"Bring a five dollar bill and drop it on the bar, and you will become a friend," said the owner.

Dale got to his feet and dug the money out of his pocket. He walked over and placed it on the bar. Having done that, the owner opened a bottle of beer and slid it down the bar towards Dale.

"Hey, are you old enough to drink?" the bar owner asked.

"How old do you have to be?"

"Twenty one."

"Then I'm old enough."

"You ain't one of them government guys trying to catch me selling beer to minors, are you?"

"Do I look like a government guy?"

The bar owner hesitated. "Good point," he said and turned to one of the men sitting at the bar.

Dale took a seat at one of the tables. It was far enough away from the overhead lights that put him in complete darkness. He gulped his beer and set the bottle on the table. It tasted good. It tasted good enough that he knew he was going to need more than one bottle. He smiled as he remembered the first time he had ever tasted a beer. It was the neighbor kid, Joe Heller, who grabbed two bottles from the refrigerator. They met in Dad's garage and within minutes had gulped them down. Dale laughed aloud as he remembered how difficult it was to even walk away from the garage. After that day, life seemed to change for Dale. It seemed that everything he did was wrong. Joe Heller went on to become a doctor, but Dale could not even hold a job. Some things in life just didn't seem fair. He laid his head down on the table and went to sleep.

It was late afternoon when the bar owner walked over to Dale's table. It was littered with empty beer bottles, and Dale was deep in sleep.

"It's time for you to get out of here," said the bar owner shaking Dale's arm.

"What do you want?" asked Dale with drool dripping from his mouth.

"Time to go."

"One more beer."

"You've had enough. Now get out of here."

Dale's face turned to anger. "I said I want one more beer."

"Get out of here before I call the marshal."

Dale paused as he remembered the marshal and spending a night in the jail. He kicked the table sending the empty bottles crashing to the floor. He slowly got to his feet staring at the bar owner with cold eyes. The other men got to their feet and slowly walked over to Dale.

"I should kill your ass right now," he said pointing a finger at the man.

The other men stepped closer.

"Somebody go call the marshal," said the bar owner.

Dale continued to stare at the man for a few more moments then turned and walked out the door.

Dark clouds rolled through the sky changing the bright blue sky into a dismal foreboding day. Dale glanced at the gas gauge on his car and saw that he was nearly out of gas. He had been travelling the back roads of Wyoming for nearly the entire afternoon. He would soon be out of gas, and he had no money. It was time to get another job.

The gas gauge needle was completely buried in the E when he coasted into the parking lot of a small motel. He scanned the outside of the building. It needed maintenance. The only kind of work he had ever done was mechanical work on cars, but he was confident that he could adapt to just about anything. He got out of his car and walked in the office.

An older woman with gray hair and wearing a man's flannel shirt was standing behind the desk. The room reeked of cigarette smoke. Country music played on a radio in the backroom.

"Need a room for the night?" she asked.

"Actually, I'm looking for a job," said Dale.

The old woman smiled and slowly shook her head. "It amazes me sometimes how God works."

"What do you mean?"

"Just yesterday, after forty years of marriage, my husband left me for another woman. I'm stuck here with this run down building, and you show up looking for a job."

Dale smiled. "That is amazing."

"Know anything about fixin' broken stuff?"

"Been a mechanic all my life."

She smiled. "I once heard that there is no such thing as a coincidence. Things happen for a reason. It was God's doings that had you walk right through that door."

"So, I've got the job?"

"Can't pay you much."

"Any chance I could live here in one of the rooms until I can find a place?"

"There are over a dozen empty rooms," she said. "Take your pick."

"Thanks. I'll do that."

"We have one other worker. She changes the beds and washes the sheets. She'll be in this afternoon."

"What's her name?"

"Rachel."

"Let me go get settled in, and I'll get started," said Dale as he headed for the door.

"Sounds good," she said. "Got plenty for you to do."

It was after dark. Dale had already fixed a door lock and a lamp that didn't work. He was finished for the day and was taking the first shower he had had in the last several days. The warm water felt good on his dry skin. He spent the last few minutes just letting the water pour over his body. He turned off the water and stepped out of the shower. Unfortunately, the towel was lying on the bed. Since he was dripping wet, he carefully walked across the floor towards the bed.

Suddenly, the front door opened. There, standing in front of him was a beautiful young woman holding a set of keys in one hand. He froze in place, standing in front of her completely naked.

"Who are you?" she asked.

"My name is Dale," he said grabbing the towel. "Who are you?"

"I'm Rachel. What are you doing in here? Nobody has used this room in months. As a matter of fact, I thought it was because the hot water didn't work."

"You clean the sheets around here, don't you?"

A look of relief fell on Rachel's face. "You're the new guy, aren't you? Ethel told me about you, but she didn't tell me that you would be staying here." She paused. "Sorry about...well, you know."

Dale forced a smile. "I guess you could say you caught me in my all-togethers."

"Sorry," she muttered. "Are you from around here?"

"Not really," he said tying the towel around his waist. "Wanna drink?"

Rachel jerked her head; her eyes widened. "Pretty bold."

Dale walked over to a table and poured a drink. He then pointed at another empty glass with the bottle. "Well?"

"Sure," she said with a smile.

He stared at her as he handed her the glass. She had blue eyes and blond hair that seemed to caress her face. She was as pretty of a woman that he had ever seen. He tightened his towel with one hand as they both sat on the side of the bed.

"What brings you to our little town?" she asked.

"No reason," said Dale sipping his drink.

"What do you mean by no reason? Everyone has a reason for whatever they do."

"Not me," said Dale staring blankly at the wall. "I'm a drifter."

"So, you just travel around the country. Where do you get your money?"

"Oh, I stop every once in a while and get a job," he said. "Hell, that's why I'm here in this place. I'm broke."

"I take it you're not married," she said sipping her drink.

Dale snickered. "Not me."

"You got something against marriage?"

"Not at all," he said. "It's just that how many women would want to live a life like this?"

"Good point."

"How 'bout you? You married?" he asked.

"I was right up until I found out what a jerk he was," she said. "You know, I'm convinced that couples should live together for a while before they get married. When they're dating they're on their best behavior. By the time you see the real person behind that smile, it's too late."

Dale gulped down the rest of his drink. He grabbed the bottle and poured himself another. He turned to Rachel and pointed the bottle at her. She finished hers and set the bottle down in front of him.

"I think you've got something there," he said filling her glass. "Dating is one thing, paying bills and washing underwear is another."

Rachel grabbed her forehead. "Wow! What's in that drink? I'm already getting a buzz."

"It's pretty strong stuff," he said staring at the label. "I'm feeling it too."

Rachel turned and stared at Dale's face. She had a partial grin and a wide-eyed look. "You got scary eyes," she blurted with slurred words.

"That's what they tell me," he said sipping his drink.

"They're so dark," she said.

Dale turned and faced her. "I've been told I have the eyes of the devil."

She paused as she reexamined him. "Eyes of the devil, you say...yes, I'd say that whoever told you that was correct." She set her glass on the table beside the bed. "I can't believe I just said that. I must be totally drunk."

"Don't feel bad," he said looking away. "You're not the first woman to tell me that I'm ugly."

Rachel picked up her glass and finished her drink. "Oh, no. I didn't say that," she said slurring every word. "You, in fact, are quite handsome. It's just those eyes. While we're at it, what about me? What do you think of me?"

Dale turned towards her. "I think you're very..."

Rachel stretched out her hands and thrust out her chest. "I got pretty big boobs, don't you think?"

Dale glanced at her chest. "Well, I'd say they are..."

"Hey, I've got a great idea," she blurted. "Let's play a game. I'll bet you I can make that towel of yours stick straight up."

"What?"

"I'll make that towel look like it has a pole under it, and I won't touch you at all."

Dale glanced at his crotch and then turned to her. "Go for it."

Rachel gulped her drink and turned to face Dale. She smiled and bent forward revealing her breasts. "You mean you didn't have any fantasies about looking down my dress?"

Dale glanced at the gaping top of her dress. Her breasts looked tanned and silky smooth. They were full and looked firm to the touch. Rachel jerked her body sending them lightly swaying beneath her.

"Good Lord," muttered Dale from a trance-like state. He took a deep breath and wiped his forehead.

Rachel slid back her chair. "Maybe you might want to see my legs, and since I don't wear underwear..." She then pulled her dress up to her thighs.

Dale glanced down at her legs. They were long and lean. She had pulled her dress up to her hips, but a fold of it drooped between her legs. His head was throbbing, his hands shaking. He wanted desperately to reach over and rip her dress from her body. Rachel took his hand and gently placed it on her leg just above the knee. Her skin was soft, and yet he could feel lean muscles.

"I think I see movement under your towel," she said, her words slurring from the drinks.

Dale said nothing. Beads of sweat formed on his forehead. Slowly, she pulled his hand further up her leg. He could feel wispy hairs touching the back of his fingers. He could feel blood pounding through his veins. He was so close. So close. Just a flinch, and he would be touching it. She was so beautiful, so sexy. He never dreamed he would ever have a chance with a woman this beautiful.

"Go ahead and touch it," she said with a soft almost throaty voice.

Dale gripped her leg in an effort to keep himself from doing it.

She leaned back and spread her legs.

"Good Lord," he muttered and tightened his grip on her leg.

"I don't think I ever saw a man with more self-control," she said. She then took his hand and gently placed it between her legs. He was panting now trying to catch his breath. He could feel the soft, warm skin at his fingertips. His index finger slipped between the folds of skin and buried deep inside her. She arched her back and moaned. Slowly, he pushed it in-and-out, Rachel moaning with every thrust. He pulled his drenched finger out and softly massaged the tender skin around the opening. Within moments, Rachel grew silent, and her legs rigid. She leaned back and spread her legs even further. Dale picked up the pace rubbing his finger back and forth over the sensitive area stopping for only a moment to lubricate his finger by thrusting it inside her. He applied more pressure and could now feel her legs quivering. She was gasping for air.

Then it happened. Rachel had held back as long as she could and finally relaxed and let it happen. She screamed in total ecstasy. As her body relaxed, Dale slowed his pace. He stopped as her body went limp.

"Oh, God!" she muttered, her eyes still closed. "Where did you learn to do that?"

"I can't really..."

"That was perfect," she said. "Most men don't have a clue."

"I'm happy that you..."

Rachel sat up straight and stared him in the eyes. "Now it's your turn," she said and got to her feet. She took two steps backward staggering from the drinks. She paused for a moment, then slipped one of the straps from her sundress over her shoulder. It fell to her waist nearly exposing one of her breasts. She slowly picked up the other strap and slid it over her other shoulder. It fell to her upper arm leaving her dress still clinging to her firm and taut breasts.

"Oh, God," muttered Dale as he watched her hand slowly move to the top of the dress. He was nearly in pain as he watched this beautiful creature unmercifully tease him. With two fingers, she picked up the dress and eased it over her breasts. It fell to her waist exposing her upper body. She quickly slipped her arms out of the straps, and the dress fell to the floor. She was completely naked except for the high-heeled strap summer shoes she was wearing.

Dale had had enough. He got to his feet and came at her with a look of determination. He took her into his arms and kissed her long and hard. His parted lips then moved to one side of her face, his lips lightly touching her cheek. They soon found her ear and lightly caressed the lobe. "I've got to have you," he whispered in her ear. She moaned in agreement. His lips ran down the side of her neck and moved to her chest. Slowly and with a gentle touch, he ran his parted lips over one of her breasts then lightly kissing the underside of it. Rachel was moaning loudly and squirming from one leg to the other.

Dale scooped her up in his arms and gently laid her on the bed. She squirmed in anticipation as he pulled his tee shirt over his head and dropped his shorts to the floor. He slipped into bed and took her in his arms. It felt good to feel her naked body against his. A flood of teenage fantasies ran through his mind. It didn't seem possible that this could be happening. All those years wasted when he could have had the one thing he desired the most.

He kissed her with all the soul and passion of his being. His tongue darted in and out of her mouth with such a steady beat that it served as a prelude of what was to come. He gently ran his fingertips down her side, over her hips and down her leg. He then ran them very slowly up the inside of her slightly parted legs, pausing to lightly circle the small patch of hair between her legs. She couldn't stand much more. Her body ached for him. There had been men in the past who could excite her, but this man had her on fire.

He pulled his lips away from hers and once again slowly dragged them across her soft cheek, down her neck and onto her chest. Her nipples were hard and as big as she had ever seen them. She ached for him to touch them. It was if they were screaming for him to grab them and put them in his mouth. Instead he ran his parted lips around the girth of her breasts being careful not to touch her nipples. It seemed cruel to her, almost as if he were torturing her. Why didn't he grab her? She ached for his firm touch. Her loins throbbed in time with her racing heartbeat. She could feel his rock hard manhood against her leg. Why didn't he use it? Why didn't he take her like some kind of animal?

Dale slid down in the bed. He then ran the tip of his tongue slowly down her side and across her flat stomach. Her legs sprung open as he rolled over between them. He put his face between her legs and lightly ran his tongue on either side of the patch of blond hair. She squirmed, uncontrollably, but held her position for him. With his two thumbs, he gently pulled back the folds of skin and ran his tongue over the tender skin inside. Rachel arched her back and gave out a loud moan.

Slowly at first, he ran his tongue over the top of the opening. She was nearly bouncing on the bed by then making it difficult for him to perform. He picked up the pace, flicking the area with the tip of his tongue. Moments later, her legs stiffened, her toes curled as her hips lifted straight up seemingly elevated out of the bed.

Her second orgasm came almost as fast as her first. This time she made no attempt to hold back. She screamed at the top of her voice. Her legs violently shook and shuddered. Her whole body seemed possessed. Dale slightly backed away. He had seen women having orgasms before but nothing like this. Moments later, she fell silent. Her hips dropped back into the bed, and her legs relaxed.

She was exhausted and spent, but Dale wasn't finished. He crawled up between her legs. He cupped one hand under her buttock and slightly lifted her off the bed. With an almost animal force, he slipped his hard member past her drenched lips and thrust it deep inside her. This time her moan was nearly a scream. He was a man obsessed. He had paid his dues. She was obviously satisfied. Now it was his turn.

It all ended in a fireball of pleasure and desire. His was a low, almost primal growl as she screamed with her third orgasm. They paused for a moment, then collapsed on the bed in complete exhaustion. Nothing was said. They lay there for several moments catching their breath and wiping sweat from their faces.

"I need a joke," she said at last.

"Huh?"

"I need to laugh."

Dale leaned on one elbow. "What in the world…"

"You wouldn't understand. Just tell me a joke."

Dale paused. "Do you know how to make a woman scream a second time after sex?"

"No. How?"

"Wipe your dick on the curtains."

Rachel started to laugh. Soon she was laughing hysterically and was choking for air.

"It wasn't that funny," said Dale with a look of shock.

Within a few moments, Rachel began to relax. She wiped the tears from her eyes. "It's a girl thing. There are times in my life when I'm so happy I need to scream or laugh hysterically, and I guarantee three orgasms will get me there."

There were several moments of silence as they stretched out on the bed. Rachel turned to Dale. His eyes were closed.

"Are you awake?" she whispered. He said nothing. He did not move. She rolled her head back over and went to sleep.

The next morning brought sunlight streaming through the windows. Rachel grabbed her forehead as she swung her feet around and set them on the floor.

"Oh, my God," she muttered. "My head hurts."

Dale was already dressed and sitting in a chair near the bed. "Maybe a bit too much to drink?"

"You're already up?" she asked.

"Been up."

She stared blankly at him as she remembered last night. "Oh, my God! I don't believe I did what I did!"

"Well, you did it," said Dale with a smile. "And I'm glad you did."

"You must think I'm a whore. I just cannot believe I did something like that to a stranger."

"I think you are someone who likes to have fun and cannot handle alcohol very well," said Dale.

Rachel massaged her head with both hands. "Well, you got the alcohol part right."

"I know this sounds like I got this a bit backwards, but I'm going to ask you anyway...wanna go out with me?"

Rachel laughed aloud. "On a date?"

Dale smiled. "Some people call it that."

"Weren't you supposed to take me out on a date with the hopes of someday doing what we did last night?"

Dale got to his feet. "Well?"

"Yeah, sure."

"I'll take you out to dinner," he said walking to the door. "Right now, I gotta get some work done."

"See ya," she said as he closed the door.

It was nearly seven in the evening when Dale stopped in front of Rachel's apartment. She walked out to his car and leaned in the window.

I have a better idea," she said. "Neither one of us can afford a night out. How would you like dinner at my place? Nothing fancy but a bit cheaper."

Dale reached over and turned off the engine. "Sounds good," he said and got out of his car.

It was a small apartment with very little furnishings. It was quite obvious that she was a meticulous house cleaner. Everything was in its place, and there were no signs of dirt anywhere.

"You have a nice place here," said Dale.

"Nothing fancy," she said. "But it's a place to hang my hat as they say."

"Something smells good."

"Have a seat. Hope you like hamburgers and French fries."

"One of my favorites," he said taking a seat.

Rachel slid a plate full of food in front of him, and then sat bottles of ketchup and mustard on the table. "Dig in."

"Do you know how long it has been since I've sat down to a regular meal in a nice place like this? I can't thank you enough."

Rachel sat down across from Dale. "Well, you must admit we're more than just casual friends."

"You know, I was thinking about last night, and I believe I owe you an apology," he said taking a bite from his sandwich.

"Why is that?"

"Let's face it. I got you drunk and took advantage of you."

"No, you didn't," she said with a stern voice. "If anything, I took advantage of you. I appreciate what you're saying, but let's face it; we both had a good time. I wouldn't change one minute of it."

Dale smiled. "Glad to hear it."

There was a pause as they both ate their food.

"So, tell me about yourself," she said. "Who is Dale Marlowe? Where did he come from and where is he going?"

"Ain't much to tell," he muttered.

"You don't talk much, do you?"

"Hell, I probably said more words to you yesterday than I've said in the past year."

"Why is that?"

"Ain't got nothing to say."

"Everybody likes to talk."

"Not me."

"Who are you?" she asked with a look of concern. "What do you do?"

Dale leaned back in his chair. "I guess I'm what you would call a drifter. Most of my life has been spent bumming rides and going from here to there. I got no purpose in life. I got a car now. Sometimes, I think I'd rather hitch hike. It's a lot cheaper."

"Where do you stay for the night? Where do you sleep?"

"You'd be surprised at how many people leave their cars unlocked," he said with a smile.

"Don't you ever get caught?"

"Oh, yeah. It happens, but jail cells ain't so bad. Got a roof over my head, a cot to sleep on and three squares."

Rachel took a bite of her sandwich and set it back down. "Wow! I don't think I've ever met anyone quite like you."

"Ain't that many people like me," he said. "Thank God."

"What do you like to do? What makes you happy?"

"Nothing."

"Come on. Everybody has something they like to do," she said.

"Not me."

"Okay. Tell me this. What would you like to do? What is your goal in life? How do you want people to remember you when you're gone?"

Dale said nothing. He stared at the floor.

Rachel bent over to stare into his eyes. "Dale?"

"Oh, people are going to remember me," he said in a cold manner.

"How so, Dale? What do you plan to do that people will remember you?"

"Can't say," he muttered.

"Sometimes you are a mystery to me," she said. "I don't know whether to be scared of you or adore you."

Dale smiled and turned towards Rachel. "You have nothing to worry about."

"So, what you're saying is that there are people in this world who need to worry," she said with a concerned voice.

Dale got to his feet. "I've got something I must do."

"Oh, sorry to hear that," said Rachel. "I thought you might be interested in a drink or two."

"Gotta go," he said and walked out the door.

For years it was called Joe's Bar and Grill then when the grill was closed, that part of the sign was removed. It was an old building with creaky floors and a strong odor of cigarette smoke.

Dale sat at a small table in the far corner of the bar. It had been nearly two hours since he had left Rachel's apartment. Empty beer bottles were scattered across his table.

"You're one serious drinker," said the bar tender as he set another beer in front of Dale.

"Take some of these God damn empties when you go," said Dale.

"Hope you got money to pay for all these," said the bar tender as he grabbed an armful of empties.

"Just keep 'em coming, for God's sakes."

Dale gulped his beer and set the bottle down on his table. He grabbed his head and closed his eyes. Images of earlier years raced through his mind. There were memories he wished would stay hidden. It was 1952, and Dale was only six years old. He tried desperately to keep up with his mother as she rapidly walked the sidewalk towards the downtown area of their small town. She needed a few groceries; no more than she could carry the few blocks to her home.

She turned to young Dale who was running in an effort to catch up.

"Hurry up, you little bastard," she barked.

"I'm going as fast as I can," he muttered with a breathless voice.

"That's your opinion. Now, run faster." She picked up her speed and turned once again. "Faster! Faster, you little shit!"

Dale was nearly out of breath. He stopped and bent over to grab his knees.

His mother stopped in frustration and walked back to stand beside her son.

"You are the most worthless piece of shit I've ever known," she said bending over. "You can't even keep up with a woman.

Hope you're proud of yourself. You were a mistake six years ago, and I now wish that I had aborted your ass."

She grabbed his ear with one hand and began to drag him down the sidewalk. Young Dale screamed as blood seeped from his ear. She dragged him for several blocks until a neighbor saw her. She dropped him to the ground and walked on.

Dale emptied his beer bottle and slammed it on the table. He softly caressed his ear, stood then staggered out of the building.

Two

It had been a rough winter with snow falling most every day and temperatures dipping below the freezing point. Ervin Meyers rolled out of bed and placed his bare feet on the cold floor. He lightly rubbed his bald head trying to ease the pain of a hangover from the previous night.

Erv had been a police officer for most of his life. After serving for nearly thirty years, he retired and returned to a small farming community called Prospect which is nestled in the flatlands of the state of Ohio. Erv spent his childhood years in Prospect and was lucky enough to buy the house that he lived in when he was growing up.

He married his childhood sweetheart. The marriage lasted nearly twenty years but came to an end when his wife found another man. Erv always blamed himself for the failed marriage. Because of his job, he was always coming and going, which made it almost impossible to make plans. It was his devotion to his job that led to her frustration and ultimate request for a divorce.

Erv slipped on a bathrobe and walked into the living room. It was nearly two in the afternoon and his favorite show was about to come on. He turned on the television and leaned back in his chair. There on the coffee table was a half empty bottle of vodka from the night before. "Ah, what the hell," he muttered and poured himself a drink.

Nearly an hour later, there was an empty bottle of vodka and a knock on the door. Erv stumbled out of his chair and managed to open the door.

"Jesus Christ, Erv! You're drunk already?" said the man as he walked inside.

"What the hell do you want, Kramer?" asked Erv as he sat back down in his chair.

Kramer Meyers was Erv's younger brother. He grew up in the small town of Prospect and became a farmer. He was a handsome man with stylish gray hair and a strong build.

"Well, I thought I would come over here and see how you are doing," said Kramer.

"Okay, you've seen me. Now, why don't you get the hell out of here?"

"Boy, you're in a good mood," muttered Kramer.

"I had a wife telling me for twenty years that I was an alcoholic; I don't need you to take up where she left off."

"Well, you are an alcoholic, aren't you?'

"Not really," said Erv draining the last of the vodka. "Alcoholics go to meetings. I'm a drunk. I go to parties."

Kramer laughed, and then stared at the empty bottle. "Got any more of that shit?"

Without saying a word, Erv reached around to the side of his chair and brought a full bottle to the coffee table. "What did you expect from a drunk?"

"Should have known," said Kramer picking up a dirty drinking glass off the floor. "What kind of diseases are in this glass?"

Erv leaned over and poured vodka into his glass. "None. Alcohol kills germs and shit."

Kramer sipped his drink. "Wow! That stuff is strong!"

"It will get ya to where you're going in a hurry."

"You said it, brother."

"So, tell me," said Erv. "Why did you come over here? I can't believe you came over here to check on me."

"Actually, that is exactly why I came over here," said Kramer. "The word around town is that you are an alcoholic. There have been many who have seen you staggering and stumbling. It's a small town, Erv. Word gets around."

"That's the one thing I miss about the city. People don't give a good God damn who you are or what you are doing. People in these small towns have their noses in everybody's business."

Kramer sipped his drink. "It would appear that your retirement isn't going well."

"Why do you say that?" asked Erv.

"All you ever do is drink and watch television. What kind of life is that?"

"One that I enjoy."

"Is it because of the divorce or nothing to do?" asked Kramer.

"What?"

"Are you unhappy because of your divorce or the fact that you have nothing to do?"

"In the first place, losing Aggie was the best thing that ever happened to me. She was a big pain in the ass. And having nothing to do is what retirement is all about, isn't it?"

"By the way, how is Aggie?" asked Kramer.

"Who knows and who cares? She married that guy she was doing. Hope he gets some 'cause I sure didn't."

"You weren't getting any?" Kramer asked. "You never told me that."

"It's nothing to be proud of," said Erv as he poured himself another drink. "Hell, I wasn't asking for anything weird. I can seriously remember going from one New Year's Eve to another and thinking there goes another year that I didn't get laid."

"I never would have guessed that of Aggie," said Kramer. "Often times, she talked dirty. Actually, acted kinda sleazy sometimes."

"Acted is the key word," said Erv.

"Well, Erv, you gotta do something. You'll go crazy if you do nothing but drink and watch television. If you had to do one thing, what would it be?"

Erv paused. "Well, the last few years of my being a cop, they had me doing investigations, and I really liked that. I often thought that I would love to do more of that kind of work."

Kramer smiled. "What d'ya mean? You want to be a private investigator?"

"Yeah, something like that."

"I hope you have improved over the years," said Kramer.

"Why? What are you talking about?"

"I remember when we were kids, and you accused me of stealing your pocket knife. Good Lord, you made my life miserable for the longest time. You were snooping through all my stuff. You told mom and dad that I had stolen the damn thing. As I recall, we even got into a fist fight over the thing, and then one day you found it in one of your boots."

Erv laughed. I'll bet if the truth was known, you were the one who put it there."

Kramer got to his feet and walked to the door. "Guess you'll never know the truth to that one."

"You did it, didn't you? You put that knife in my boot!" shouted Erv as he pointed a finger.

Kramer smiled as he walked out the door. "See you later."

ᏗᏗᏗ

It was early afternoon when Dale staggered out the door of his motel room. His scheduled time to begin work was eight o'clock in the morning, and it was now after two in the afternoon. To make matters worse, Dale was so intoxicated that he could hardly walk. He managed to walk the length of the building then burst open the office door.

"Hey, there, Ethel," he said staggering across the floor.

"Where have you been?" she asked. "You were supposed to report for work at eight o'clock this morning."

Dale leaned on her desk. His face was only inches away from hers. "I overslept."

"You're drunk!" she shouted.

"Oh, no I'm not. I'm just a little bit drowsy. That's all."

"I'm not that stupid," she said. "What are you doing coming in here this late in the day and drunk on top of it?"

"Why? Is that a problem?"

"Well, I never!" she said with a look of amazement.

"Well, maybe you should," he said with a smile. "After all, you ain't that bad looking."

"How dare you to talk to me that way."

"How do you want me to talk to you?" he asked still smiling.

"That's it! You're fired!"

Dale's smile disappeared. "What did you say?"

"I said you're fired. Now, get out of here."

"You can't fire me for being late!"

"I just did," she said. "Now, once again, get out of here."

Dale stepped towards Ethel with his fists doubled, then stopped. The thought of losing Rachel from the consequences of what he was about to do flashed through his brain. He turned and started for the door.

"Bitch!" he shouted as he walked out the door.

It was nearly six o'clock when Dale stumbled in the back door. He fell into a chair in the kitchen and leaned his head back against the wall.

"Looks like you had a bad day," said Rachel as she sat down at the table. "Somehow I don't think it is from working hard."

"The bitch fired my ass," muttered Dale. "Can you believe it?"

"Why did she fire you?"

"I was late coming to work. Is that any reason for getting fired? Hell, it was the first time I ever done that."

"Why were you late?"

"Overslept."

"How late were you?"

"Oh, I don't remember. I'm sure it wasn't all that bad. Doesn't seem fair. I'm late one time, and the bitch fires me."

"What are you going to do now?"

Dale leaned forward in his chair. "I'm not sure. Probably look for another job."

"Finding another job might be harder than you think," she said.

"Why is that?"

"Well, in the first place there aren't that many jobs out there," she said. "In the second place, this is a small town. Word spreads fast. By tomorrow, everyone in town will know what happened to you and your job."

Dale paused. "What do I do now?"

Rachel smiled. "I guess you're just going to have to move in with me."

Dale turned and stared at her. "Are you kidding?"

"No, I'm not kidding," she said with an awkward look on her face. "I've...I've fallen in love with you and want you with me all the time."

Dale reached across the table and took her hand. "I can't believe it," he said with a smile.

"You can't believe what?"

"I can't believe you are in love with me," he said with a surprised look.

"Why is that so hard to believe?"

"Well, for one reason, we just met not too awful long ago."

"I know," she said. "I know this isn't normal, but I fell in love with you the first moment I met you. I think you're the one who was meant for me. I love you, Dale Marlowe."

Dale softly grabbed her arm and pulled her close to him. He wrapped his arms around her and kissed her softly on the lips.

"What makes this such a surprise is I was going to tell you the same thing," he said backing away. "I fell in love with you from the moment I met you."

Rachel's face glowed. "It's as if fate brought us together."

"I know this all seems so strange," said Dale. "People don't just fall in love at the drop of a hat, but I can't help it."

Rachel's smile grew larger as she slowly shook her head. "I just can't believe this is happening to me. I've had so many problems in the past that you'd think I would be a little more careful."

"Well, I really do believe we should give it some time," said Dale with a sober look on his face. "Let's not rush into anything."

"Yes…yes, you're right," said Rachel. "We should not rush into anything. If it was meant to be, it will happen."

"I've seen too many couples rush into things and regret it later," said Dale. "I think couples should live together for a while before they make the big move. There's a big difference between dating and a life of paying bills and washing dirty underwear."

There was a long pause.

"What should we do now?" Rachel asked.

Dale grabbed her by the arm. "Let's go to bed and think this over."

人 人 人

Months passed, and for the first time in Dale's life, he was happy. He found a new job washing dishes in the local restaurant. The only reason he was able to acquire a job after being fired from the motel was the owner was Rachel's cousin. Washing dishes was not what Dale wanted to do, but he was willing to make any sacrifice to have a life with Rachel. He had never been happier in his life, and he was determined to do whatever he had to do to make it happen.

Horrible memories of his childhood that haunted him every day had for the first time in his life disappeared. The chronic hatred that he had for his now departed mother was slowly dissipating. It was if he had started a new life, a life that was filled with joy. Unfortunately, Dale could not stop his drinking, and because Rachel was now drinking nearly as much as he was, she offered no discouragement.

It was early one Saturday morning. Rachel rolled over and wrapped her arms around Dale. He pulled her close until their naked bodies were one.

"Sleep good?" she asked.

"I sure did. How 'bout you?"

"Thanks to you, I slept like a dream."

"Why?" What did I do," asked Dale with a serious look on his face.

"Fantastic sex does it every time," she said. "I never really knew what good sex was like until I met you."

Dale pulled her even closer. "Glad to be of service."

"I think I'll keep you around," she said with a warm smile.

"What are we going to do today?" he asked. "Neither one of us has to work today. We should do something special."

"I know what we should do, but I doubt that you will want to."

"Well, I can't say one way or the other until you tell me," said Dale with a look of concern.

"Let's get married," she said bluntly.

Dale sat up in bed and stared at her. "What did you say?"

"I said let's get married."

"Just like that," said Dale. "You want to go get married. You make it sound like let's go get some ice cream."

"Well..."

Dale smiled. "Well, what are you waiting on?"

⋏ ⋏ ⋏

It was late afternoon when George Armstrong finished feeding the hogs and chickens. He closed the door to the barn and started for the house. George had been a farmer all his life. His father and grandfather had been farmers, and it just seemed natural for him to follow in their footsteps.

As all farmers, he spent most of his summers working in the fields planting or maintaining corn, wheat or oats. Then, as summer ended, he would harvest the fields and prepare for winter. With the fields dormant for the long winter, the only thing left was to attend to the livestock with the financial goal of selling them for the best price.

George opened the backdoor and stepped inside the enclosed porch. He bent over and removed his boots so as to not infuriate his wife, Martha.

"Is supper ready?" George asked as stepped into the kitchen.

Martha was bent over the stove. "Did you take your boots off?" she asked without turning around.

"Yes, dear," he said closing the door behind him.

"By the time you get your hands washed, supper will be ready," she said.

George quickly washed his hands and returned to the kitchen.

"You couldn't have used soap," she said as she set a bowl of food on the table. "You weren't in there long enough."

"They weren't that dirty in the first place," said George spreading his hands open.

"Well, go ahead and sit down. Supper won't wait."

He grabbed a bowl of mashed potatoes and spooned a pile onto his plate. "I hear that rich people in the city call this meal their dinner."

"Well, we ain't rich and as far as that goes who cares what you call it as long as it tastes good."

"Can't argue with that," said George sticking a forkful of food in his mouth. "By the way, where's our son?"

"Arthur is at the library looking up something for school," she said. "He will be home a little later."

"All the more food for me," said George.

"Got a birthday card from Rachel," she said. "I get a card from her and she lives clear out in Wyoming. Wouldn't you think I would get a card, a call or anything from my son who lives a few blocks away?"

"Here we go again," said George rolling his eyes. "Every year we go through this."

"Well? Is that asking too much?"

"You know as well as I do that guys are terrible about things like that. Women are much more thoughtful than men. It's just the way things are."

"That's no excuse," said Martha. "Why can't you men be a little more considerate of others?"

"Hey, don't throw me in with that bunch," said George. "I got you a birthday card."

"I'll grant you that, but it wouldn't have hurt much if you had got me a present."

"And just what would I have gotten you?"

"I leave hints all the time."

"Hints? What hints?"

"I told you the other day that I was out of perfume."

"You did not tell me such a thing."

"I did too."

"So what you are saying is that you looked me right in the eye and told me that you were out of perfume," said George with a hint of a grin. "Is that what you did?"

"Well... not exactly."

"So, you didn't tell me that at all."

"Oh, I said it. I might have said it softly."

"You mean that you might have muttered it?"

"There are those who might describe it that way."

George reached under the table and pulled out a small package wrapped in birthday gift wrap and sweetened with a bow on top. He handed it to Martha with a smile. "Happy birthday," he said.

"Oh, you old fool," she said taking the present. "I knew there was a reason I have stayed with you for all these years."

"I got you that perfume you've been using for all these years, so I'm pretty sure I got you the right one," he said. "But if not, Henry at the drugstore said you could bring it back."

Martha got out of her chair and walked over to George. She leaned over and kissed him. "I love you, George Armstrong."

"I love you too," he whispered.

入 入 入

Prospect was a small community centered in the farmlands of eastern Ohio. It was a quiet town with three grocery stores, four gas stations, two hardware stores and one drugstore. In spite of the town's serene, almost Norman

Rockwell look about it, it did have a liquor store. There was much controversy and outrage when it opened, and much talk of boycott, and, yet, in time, it became one of the most prosperous and productive stores in town.

Kramer Meyers pulled his car into a parking space in front of the liquor store only to find his brother exiting the store with armloads of purchases.

Kramer stuck his head out of the window. "Expecting the entire U. S. Marine Corp. to stop by?"

Erv paused as he glanced at his brother. "Hey, give me a ride back to my place," he said. He then opened the side door and shoved the bags of bottles into the car.

"Good Lord," said Kramer. "What the hell is that all about?"

"Buford has a clearance sale going on," said Erv. "He said something about some of his stuff getting old."

Kramer smiled. "I thought liquor got better as it aged."

"This is stuff that has been sitting around and not selling."

"In other words, it's shitty stuff," said Kramer.

"Maybe to some people, but to me it's alcohol and will get me to where I want to be."

"Man, you have a problem," said Kramer. "You need help."

"I sure do, and I gotta thank you. I never would have got this stuff home if it hadn't been for you."

Kramer slowly shook his head as he backed out of the parking space. "Hey, didn't you mention something about becoming a private eye?"

"Yeah. Why?"

"I was reading in the newspaper about a retired cop who became a private eye. He makes a butt load of money, and about all he does is track down some guy who is cheating on his wife."

"Oh, couldn't do that."

"Why not?"

"It would cut into my drinking time," said Erv. "Besides, there's probably a reason these guys are out there trying to get laid."

"Well, not getting any at home doesn't make it right," said Kramer.

"Doesn't make it wrong either."

"Anyways, I just thought you might be interested in making a few extra bucks by doing that private eye stuff," said Kramer.

"Oh, I am but not right now," said Erv. "I just want to enjoy not having to go to work. Do you know that of all the years I was a cop, I never called in sick. Not even once."

"That's incredible."

"Of course, that and a buck will get you a cup of coffee."

"I saw Aggie the other day," said Kramer. "She was with her boyfriend."

Erv smiled. "That poor bastard. He actually thinks he is going to get laid for the rest of his life. He hasn't seen the married Aggie. I was wondering why she had such a big smile on her face when she was walking down the aisle to get married. She was thinking that she never have to do that again."

"Wonder what kind of problem she had," said Kramer.

"Well, as we are walking into the court room to get a divorce, she tells me that her stepfather raped her. Maybe, if she had told me that a bit sooner, we could have gotten her some help."

"As I recall, your trip inside that courtroom wasn't your best day, was it?"

"No shit," said Erv. "I catch her screwing another guy, and she gets the house, half of my pension and I get to fork over alimony every month. Why in God's name do we ever get married in the first place is beyond me."

Kramer pulled into Erv's driveway and stopped at the front door. Erv got out and wrapped his arms around the bags of liquor.

"Need any help?" Kramer asked.

"I could use some help drinking all this."

Kramer shifted into reverse. "Maybe later."

Erv closed the door and watched as he drove away.

Three

The early morning sunlight drifted through the window sending playful-looking shadows on the walls and ceiling. Rachel opened her eyes and smiled as she stared at them. It had been several weeks since they had been married, and she had never been happier. Dale was moody and would sometimes go into a depressive state that would last for hours, but she would dismiss such actions as simply a mood swing.

Dale rolled over and smiled. "Morning, Mrs. Marlowe."

Rachel gave him a quick kiss. "Morning, Mr. Marlowe. Sleep well?"

"After what you did for me last night, who wouldn't?"

Rachel paused. "I've been thinking."

Dale sniffed several times. "I thought I smelled something burning."

"Oh, you," she said with a smile. "I have something I want to ask you."

Dale sat up in bed. "Fire away."

"I want to go back home to Ohio."

"Well, we really can't afford a vacation right now," said Dale with a sober look.

"I'm not talking about a vacation. I want to go back to Ohio to live.

Dale sat straighter and turned to Rachel. "Why would you want to do that?"

"I miss my family for one thing," she said with a sad voice. "Besides, I really don't like it out here."

"What's not to like about this wide open country out here?"

"All you have out here are flatlands and deserts," she said. "I'm a city girl. Well, I come from small town, but I like Ohio, and I really miss my family."

"Where would we live back there? We don't have any money. We're just getting by as it is."

"I already have an idea of where we could live," said Rachel rubbing her hands together. "My father owns a small trailer near his house. I'm sure he would let us live there until we could get on our feet."

"Do you really think he would let us live there?"

"I'll call him to be sure, but I can tell you that he will be overjoyed that we would be coming home."

Dale paused as he thought about what she had just said. "Well, then, let's go call him."

It was a long journey from Wyoming to Ohio, one that Dale really didn't want to make. He particularly loved the western states. He, in fact, spent most of his adulthood roaming, aimlessly, across that part of the country. If it had been anybody but Rachel, he would have denied such a request, but in spite of his true feelings, he agreed to go.

Because of their limited finances, they couldn't afford to rent a truck to transport their belongings, so they packed as much as they could aboard Dale's car and took off. Unfortunately, they left behind nearly all of Rachel's furniture and utilities. Nearly everything that was loaded into the car was clothes and a small amount of food. Everything else was, regrettably, left behind.

It was nearly a week before they finally reached the small town of Prospect, Ohio. Evening was approaching as they pulled into the driveway. George and Martha were settled in for the night when they heard an older model car pull in and park beside their house.

"My goodness! That must be Rachel and her new husband," said Martha as she started for the door. "And I want you to behave, Mr. Armstrong. This new husband has to be better than her first one."

"Well, I'll give you that one," said George. "Nobody could be worse than that bastard."

"George! Watch your mouth! We have company walking up to our front door. Behave yourself."

"The price you gotta pay just to see your daughter," George muttered.

As they approached the house, Martha opened the front door. Martha opened her arms and wrapped them around Rachel.

"Oh, Mother, I've missed you so much," said Rachel with tears in her eyes.

"It's so nice to see you again," said Martha.

Rachel turned to her father and hugged him as well.

"Oh, my God, Dad! I missed you too," she said.

"It's been a long time, kid," he said taking her in his arms.

Martha glanced at Dale and then turned to Rachel. "I hate to break this up, but I think you need to introduce us to the groom."

Rachel turned and pulled Dale next to her.

"Dale, this is my father, George, and my mother, Martha. Mom and Dad, this is Dale."

"Glad to meet you," they said in unison.

"I've heard a lot about you folks," said Dale as he shook George's hand.

"I hope it was all good," said Martha.

"Oh, yes. She speaks very highly of you folks."

Rachel turned and glanced down the hallway. "Where's Billy?"

"He's over at his friend's house right now," said Martha. "Something to do with his homework."

"That's your brother?" Dale asked.

"That would be him," said Rachel. "He's hardly ever at home."

"Would you two like to sit a spell?" George asked. "I'll bet you could use a strong drink."

Rachel stepped forward. "Actually, we've had a long day and could really use some sleep."

"Oh, yes, by all means," said George digging in his pocket. "Here's the key to the trailer. You know where it is."

As they turned to leave, Dale stopped and turned back to face George. "Any chance I could get that stiff drink that you mentioned?"

"Sure," said George heading towards the kitchen. "I'll be right back."

"I can't believe you did that," said Rachel.

"Did what?"

"Asked my dad for a drink. Isn't it enough that he is letting us live in his trailer?"

"Hey, we've been driving for miles," said Dale. "I could use a drink."

"Here you go," said George carrying a bottle of whiskey. "Take the whole bottle."

"Well, thank you, Mr. Armstrong," said Dale. "I'm afraid I don't have any money to…"

"Don't think a thing about it," said George. "Call it a welcoming gift or, better than that, call it a wedding gift."

"I really appreciate this, Mr. Armstrong," said Dale.

"It's George to you, son."

Dale paused as he took in what was said. "Well, thank you…George."

"Go get some sleep, you two. You both look exhausted."

"Good night, Dad," said Rachel as she closed the door.

It was a long walk across the backyard, garden and a spot near a wooded area. It was a small trailer that was nearly fifty years old. Rust streamed down the sides, and it leaned to one side as if it would soon fall over. They both stopped in front of it and stared at the outside condition.

"If it looks this bad out here, I can't imagine what the inside looks like," said Dale.

"I remember playing inside when I was a kid," said Rachel. "I don't remember it being all that bad."

"How long ago was that?"

"At least twenty years ago."

"Open 'er up," said Dale. "Let's see how much work we have ahead of us."

Rachel unlocked the door, and they both stepped inside. Dale ran his hand over the wall until he found a switch then turned it on. The interior was small and in complete decay. What little furniture remained needed desperately to be replaced, and there was a stench in the air that seemed to permeate throughout the trailer.

"What is that smell?" Rachel asked.

"Smells like rotten food," said Dale as he opened the refrigerator.

"Good God!" shouted Rachel. "What is that in there?"

"I don't know, but it's all yours," he said pulling the package out of the refrigerator. He then opened the door and threw it outside.

They paused as they studied the interior.

"Let's get some sleep and start on this place in the morning," said Rachel.

"Sounds like a plan," said Dale as they headed for the bedroom.

For the next several days, Dale and Rachel were busy cleaning the trailer and getting it in a livable condition. It was hard work but their efforts were rewarded with a clean and inviting interior. They decided to wait until they could afford paint before they started on the outside. It was late in the afternoon on the third day that they flopped down on the couch.

"Well, she looks pretty good from where I sit," said Rachel.

"She'll do," said Dale.

Rachel turned and stared at Dale. "What the hell is wrong with you? You've been grumpy all day."

"I need a drink."

"You always need a drink. Did anyone ever call you an alcoholic?"

Dale got up and started for the kitchen. "Call me anything you want. I'm going to have a drink."

"If you kept it to one drink that would be one thing, but drinking until you are falling on the floor is another."

"Back off," he said with a demanding voice.

"Back off? I'm just stating facts. I ain't making anything up."

Dale placed a bottle of alcohol on the kitchen table and sat down in front of it. "Just leave me alone."

"Boy, the real you is coming out of the closet," she said sarcastically. "I didn't expect you to be Mister Nice Guy all the time, but I didn't expect this."

Dale ignored the comment. He lifted the bottle of booze and gulped it down.

It was early evening when Rachel walked into the kitchen. Dale was passed out with his head lying on the table. There was one empty bottle and another one half full. He was snoring and the table near his open mouth was covered with drool. Rachel began to collect the dirty dishes and placed them in the sink.

She stopped and stared at the man sitting at the table. There was something about him that bothered her. She wasn't quite sure what it was, but she really believed there was a side of Dale Marlowe that he had kept hidden. If her hunch was right, that side of him was nothing she really wanted to see.

She reached over and lightly shook him. "Why don't you go to bed?"

Dale groaned, and then leaned back in his chair. He wiped his mouth and face with his hands. "What did you say?'

"I said why don't you go to bed?"

Dale said nothing. He stared at his empty drinking glass for several moments, and then picked up the bottle of whisky and poured another drink.

"Good Lord, Dale!" she shouted. "You can't be serious!"

Dale chugged down the drink and poured another.

"You have a serious problem, Mr. Marlowe," she said sarcastically.

"Yeah, I got a problem," he muttered. "My problem is you."

"I'm the problem? I'm the problem? Look at you. You're drunker than I've ever seen anybody get. What's the matter with you? Normal people don't do this."

Suddenly something happened to Dale. He was staring at the table when the look on his face changed to a look of fear. His eyes squinted as he grabbed the sides of his head and screamed, "Please don't do that again!"

Rachel pulled up another chair and sat down beside him. "Are you okay?" she asked with a soft voice.

Dale screamed as if he were in pain. "Please don't do that, Mother! It hurts so bad I can't stand it!" He slid back his chair and dropped to the floor. He then scooted along the floor on his knees while clutching his ears.

Rachel fell back into her chair in disbelief. "Oh, my God! Is there anything I can do for you?"

Dale soon came to a stop. He fell silent and slowly removed his hands from his ears. After a few moments, he slowly got to his feet and sat back down at the table.

"My God, Dale," said Rachel. "What was that all about?"

Dale paused as he ran his hands through his hair. "It was nothing."

"What do you mean it was nothing? That was the most frightening thing I've ever seen. Why were you bringing your mother into it?"

"She was a horrible mother," he said. "That's why."

"Oh, my God," said Rachel. "I don't think I have ever heard someone described their mother as horrible. What did she do to you?"

Dale was now staring blankly at the floor. "I don't want to talk about it."

"Talk to me, Dale," pleaded Rachel. "This is more than just a little problem. You need to get this out in the open. It would seem that you've kept this bottled up for much too long."

Dale paused for several moments. He sniffed uncontrollably and wiped tears from his eyes. "She used to beat me all the time. Never really needed a reason. She would beat me with a board until she got tired. If we were going somewhere by foot, she would grab my ear and drag me until my ear was bleeding. The only reason she would stop was to avoid others from seeing her doing it. She didn't stop because she was hurting me."

"My God," muttered Rachel. "That's the most incredible..."

"That ain't the worst," he said his voice quivering. "There was something about her that was worse than all of the beatings and ear pullings." He turned and stared Rachel in the eyes. "How would you like to have your mother tell you that she hates you and wishes you had never been born?"

Rachel jumped back in her chair. "My Lord, are you serious?"

"I could take anything she dished out but that," he said his voice shaking. "There's nothing worse in this God forsaken world."

"I feel so sorry for you. Nobody should…"

"She was drunk one night. I mean really drunk. She didn't drink much, but when she did, she was really bad. I was sixteen at the time just starting to have fun in life. Well, it all came to an end that night when she was drunk. She kicked me out and told me to never come back. I stood there looking at her. I couldn't believe what she was saying. I hadn't done anything wrong, and here she was telling me to get out. I stood there completely stunned until she came at me. There was no way I was going to stand there and let her grab my ear again, so I walked out. Didn't have a dime to my name. Didn't even have an extra pair of underwear."

"What did you do after leaving?"

"I have spent the better part of my life as a drifter. Walked most of the time. Hitchhiked from time to time. I'd get a job here and there to keep myself fed."

"Have you ever told anybody about this before telling me?"

"You're the first."

"You've kept this bottled up all these years?"

"Wasn't anybody to tell," he said wiping his eyes. "Had no friends. Never knew anybody for more than a week or two."

"You should have told the police," said Rachel. "She sounded like an evil woman who should have gone to jail."

"She would have denied it. It would have been her word against mine, and I'm sure I know how that would have gone."

"Whatever became of her?"

"Have no idea. I never went back."

"Suppose she's dead?" Rachel asked.

"Don't care," he replied with no emotions.

Rachel paused as she thought about what he had said. All of this was new to her. She had never experienced such a life. She loved and was as close to her parents as anyone could be, so to hear what Dale's life was almost frightful to her, and she really wasn't sure how to react.

"I guess...I guess I don't blame you," she said. "I can't imagine what you've been through."

"Having second thoughts about marrying me?" asked Dale.

Rachel smiled and lightly grabbed his arm. "Oh, no. That will never happen. You're mine for ever and a day."

Dale turned to her and smiled. "Come on. Let's get some sleep. It's been a long day."

The next morning, Rachel rolled over in bed to find Dale missing. She got out of bed, wrapped a nightgown around her and opened the bedroom door. As she walked towards the front of the trailer, she could see Dale sitting at the kitchen table. As she approached him, she could see he was drinking from a bottle of beer. She walked around the table and stared as he gulped more beer.

"What the hell are you doing?" she asked.

"Drinking my breakfast," he replied.

"I don't believe you."

"What's not to believe?"

"You are drinking beer at seven in the morning? Since when have you been doing that?"

"Is this a problem?"

"People don't drink beer for breakfast, for God's sakes," she said putting her hands on her hips.

"I do," he said taking another sip.

Rachel sat down at the table with a disgusted look. "You know, I talked with my brother, the one who owns an automobile repair shop, and he told me that he needs a mechanic. I told him that you might be interested. I was going to ask you to go talk with him, but I guess that won't happen today."

"Why not today?"

"You've been drinking, for Christ's sakes. You can't go interview for a job while you're drunk."

"Drunk? I'm only having two beers," said Dale.

"And that won't make you drunk?"

"I may not be too smart, but I do know my alcohol."

"Well, do you mind going down there?" she asked. "I told him you might come down there."

Dale got to his feet. "I'm on my way."

It was a short drive to the downtown area. Dale cruised the area until he found the intersection of Marsh and Vine streets, and the automobile repair shop on the corner. There were cars parked all around the building and, yet, nobody in sight. Dale parked his car and slowly walked into the shop. There was a car on a hoist and a young man standing under it.

"Hello," shouted Dale.

The young man turned to Dale. "Can I help you?"

"From the looks of things, I think I should be asking you the same thing."

The young man wiped his hand on his coveralls and shook Dale's hand. "You must be Rachel's husband."

"That would be me."

"My name is Luke."

"Nice to meet you, Luke," said Dale. "I've heard a lot about you."

"Rachel tells me that you are quite the mechanic."

"She might be exaggerating a bit to help get me a job."

"Well, as you can see, I need some help," said Luke. "When do you want to start?"

"How 'bout right now?"

Luke pointed at a doorway. "There are coveralls inside that room. Get dressed, and you can finish this one right here."

⅄ ⅄ ⅄

Nearly a month passed. Dale had been working long hours as a mechanic while Rachel spent her time cleaning and straightening their new home. It was a Saturday night, and Rachel's parents had invited them over for dinner. It was a cold December night as they walked across the open field to the Armstrong's house. Rachel had insisted that Dale stay sober for the evening which led to screaming argument. As they walked up the steps to the Armstrong's front door, they decided to put aside their differences for the evening.

Rachel tapped on the door, and then opened it.

"Well, look who's here," said George with a smile.

"Hi, Dad," said Rachel as she headed for the sofa.

George extended his hand to Dale who reluctantly took it. "How are you doing?" George asked.

"Good," Dale replied with a solemn look. He then took a seat in a chair on the opposite side of the room from Rachel.

The smile of George's face disappeared as he glanced at Rachel's face then at Dale.

"Can I interest you in a drink" George asked.

Dale turned to Rachel with a cold stare. "Yes, I would love a drink."

"How 'bout you, Rachel?" George asked.

"No thanks," she said as she turned to Dale. "I didn't come here to get drunk."

George paused for a moment then left the room. He could feel the tension but was not sure of the reason for it. He assumed that there was some kind of dissention between the newly wedded couple. Maybe a drink would do everyone some good. He walked into the kitchen and grabbed a bottle of vodka.

"Is that the kids I hear?" Martha asked.

"They're here," said George. "And not exactly in the greatest of moods."

"Have they been fighting again?"

"That's what it looks like."

"That's becoming an everyday thing with them," said Martha as she set food on the table.

"No different from when we first got married," said George. "Or any other newly wed couple. "Don't forget there is an awakening for every guy who soon realizes that he ain't the boss anymore."

"Go keep them busy, so that they don't get into it again," she said.

George grabbed the two drinks and returned to the living room.

"Here ya go," he said as he handed the drink to Dale.

Dale grabbed the drink and sipped it. "Thanks," he muttered.

George took a seat and sipped his as well. "So, Luke tells me that you're quite the mechanic."

"Been messing with cars all my life."

"What prompted you to get involved with that?" George asked.

"I don't know. Guess I was too stupid to do anything else."

"Too stupid? Good Lord, how many people have the talent to fix a car? I'd say you were anything but stupid."

"I got the grades to prove I was stupid."

"Ahhh, so you didn't know where Poland is," said George. "The important thing is you have a talent."

"Wouldn't call it a talent," Dale muttered.

"Well, anyway, I guess I don't know much about you," said George. "Are your parents still living?"

"Never really knew my dad that well, and I'm not too sure about my mother."

"You don't know whether she's alive or dead?"

"That's about right," said Dale.

"So, she left home as well?"

"Not really. She kicked my ass out."

"What the hell did you do to get kicked out of the house?"

"Don't remember."

"You still love your mother, don't you?" George asked. "Everyone loves their mother."

"Well, here's one person who doesn't," said Dale with a hardened voice.

"You don't?"

"No, sir, I don't."

"I don't think I've ever heard of such a thing," said George. "How old were you when she kicked you out?"

"I don't know. I guess I was around seventeen."

"And you don't remember why she did it?"

Dale chugged down his drink. "You're not seeing the big picture here. It wasn't just because she kicked me out. There were many other reasons."

George paused. He could see that he was heading down a road where he did not belong. He turned to Rachel. It was obvious that she was even more irate than when she first walked through the door.

"Tell you what," said George clapping his hands together and getting to his feet. "Let me go see how dinner is coming along."

As he walked out of the room, Rachel leaned forward and pointed a finger at Dale. "Why do you have to be such a jerk?"

"Why? What did I do?"

"You treated my father horribly."

"Well, he's an asshole."

"What?" shouted Rachel as she got to her feet. "What did you call my father?"

"I think you heard me. He's an asshole."

"He's not an asshole. You're the asshole."

Dale got to his feet and started for the door. "I'm out of here," he said and slammed the door behind him.

Four

It was the beginning of a new year. The winter had been relatively calm but there were still many weeks before spring. Erv had done very little since his retirement besides drinking and watching television. He had thought about and had seriously considered doing some improvements around the house but had easily dismissed it using the excuse that he was recently retired and deserved leisure time. Besides, since his divorce, he no longer had to listen to her complaints and could do just about anything he wanted to do.

One morning in early January, Erv woke to a bright and sunny morning. He opened the curtains in his living room and was amazed at how sunny it was. It was almost as if he was looking at a summer morning. He decided that it was finally time for him to get to work. He had let too many things deteriorate right in front of him. He studied the interior from wall to wall. There were beer bottles, empty packages of all sorts, and decayed food laying everywhere. Erv bent over and started to work.

It was several hours later when he had completed most of the work. He now had a roomful of filled garbage bags, and was about to begin carrying them out to the curb when the doorbell rang. Erv opened the door to find his brother standing on the porch.

"Since when did you start ringing the doorbell?" Erv asked. "You normally just open the door and walk in."

"Well, normally, that's what I do," said Kramer walking through the door. "This time, I happened to peek through your picture window and saw how clean it was. That didn't look like my brother's doings, so I figured someone else must be living here."

"Well, sir, I decided to get off my ass," said Erv with a smile.

"Wow! What prompted that?" Kramer asked as he glanced around the room.

"I don't know. I guess I got tired of doing nothing."

"So, what else are you planning to do?"

"Well, I was thinking about painting the walls in this living room," said Erv as he glanced around the room.

"You really are gung hoe, aren't you?"

"Aggie and I did nothing but argue, and one of the subjects was the color we should paint this room. We argued that one for so long that I just finally gave up. Now, I can paint it any color I want."

"What color are you going to paint it?"

"Hell, I don't know," said Erv. "Just out of spite, I might paint it the color she wanted."

"I like the way you think," said Kramer. "By the way, I got a call from Rose the other day."

"And how is our sister doing?"

"She seems to be okay," said Kramer with a disturbed look. "For some reason, she's been running back and forth to Cincinnati. Says she's looking for a job."

"So, what's wrong with that?" Erv asked.

"I don't know. I just don't like her running around in a big city. I know she's just like every other woman today who thinks they are as tough as a man, but we both know different."

"What are you talking about? There was no doubt in my mind that Aggie could have kicked my ass," said Erv.

"No, I'm serious," said Kramer. "I know I'm old school, but I don't think a woman should run around in a city by herself. There are too many bad guys and perverts out there."

"Well, I'll give you that one," said Erv. "But what are you going to do about it? You can't tell Rose to stay home."

"I know, but she worries me. Rose doesn't think about things like that. I remember when she was a teenager and went up to downtown Cleveland with some other girls. They were right down in the thick of it, and it was after dark. Hell, I wouldn't have done such a thing."

"Maybe, we should talk to her," said Erv. "She might listen if we both sit her down."

"I sincerely doubt it, but I suppose we could try."

"Wanna beer?" Erv asked.

"No, thanks. I need to get going in a minute," said Kramer. "I still think you need to do something with yourself."

"Like what?"

"I don't know. You have all those years as an investigator. You need to turn that experience into money. There is always someone who has a problem or needs to find someone. You're the man, Erv, who can help them."

"Ah, I'd rather drink beer and watch television," said Erv. "Besides, I'm doing okay on my retirement. Aggie didn't get everything."

"Gotta go, Erv. Take care."

ʎ ʎ ʎ

Weeks passed. Dale had made a strong effort to succeed at his new job not only to support his new wife but to show a certain amount of dignity to her brother. He hadn't been late for work and had made a point not to get angry or argue with his new boss. His relationship with Rachel had improved tremendously mostly because he had cut back considerably with his drinking. He still drank a few beers form now and then but not to the extreme where he would become intoxicated.

It was a cold day in January. It had been snowing all night, and the roads were deep in snow, but Dale made it to work in spite of the foul conditions. On his way into work, Dale had developed a bad habit of drinking one or two beers as he drove the distance. Generally, he had little or no effect on him, but if he had not eaten breakfast and was drinking on an empty stomach, it was very impactful. He was busy working on a car when an older man appeared. He searched the building until he found Luke then marched over to him.

"I had to walk across town to get here. Wanna know why?" the man asked.

"Well, good morning, Wilbur," said Luke. "How are you?"

"I asked you a question," said Wilbur. "Got any idea why I had to walk over here?"

"Ah...you needed the exercise?"

"Don't be a smart ass, Luke," said Wilbur. "I brought my car in because it wouldn't start. Your guy worked on it for over an hour, and then I paid all that money for what? It still doesn't start. In fact, it's sitting in my driveway as we speak."

"What did we do to your car?" asked Luke.

"Hell, I don't know. Ask your dumb ass mechanic."

Luke turned to the back of the shop. "Hey, Dale! Come here, will ya?"

There was the clang of a tool hitting the concrete floor, and then Dale stepped from behind a car that was suspended in the air on a rack.

"What's up?" Dale asked.

"That's the guy," said Wilbur pointing his finger in Dale's face. "That's the guy who screwed me over."

Dale stopped right in front of Wilbur. He towered nearly a foot over the old man. "What the hell is your problem?"

"I brought my car in here to get it fixed. You spent hours working on it. This guy over here took a shitload of money from me, and the car still doesn't start. Now, what are you going to do about it?"

"Well, if you don't simmer down, I'm going to kick your ass."

Wilbur moved even closer. "You're gonna kick my ass? Why don't you just try it, asshole?"

Dale reached up to grab the man by the neck when Luke jumped in. "Okay, that's enough both of you. Now, as for your car and its problem, I will personally take care of it."

The two men stared at each other as they slowly backed away. Luke stood between them with both arms extended in an effort to keep them apart.

"That will work for me," said Wilbur. "Just keep that jerk away from me and my car."

"Why you son-of-a-bitch!" shouted Dale. He, then, pushed Luke to the floor and attacked Wilbur. He grabbed him by the shirt with one hand and hit him in the cheek with his fist. Blood flew across Wilbur's face and onto the floor. He lost his balance and started to fall when Dale grabbed even tighter with his one hand. He then pulled his fist back and swung it with all his might. This time he connected with the man's eye sending blood splattering everywhere. Wilbur's arms dropped motionless to the floor. He was obviously unconscious. Dale released his grip on his shirt allowing the blood-soaked man to fall onto the floor.

"Good Lord, what have you done?" Luke asked as he slowly got to his feet.

"Ain't nobody gonna talk to me that way," said Dale as he stood upright. He paused for a moment then started after him again with his hands open.

"No, you don't!" shouted Luke scrambling to his feet. "You've done enough already. It looks as if you've killed him."

"Ah, he'll be alright," said Dale backing away.

"You can't do shit like this to customers."

"Well, I ain't puttin' up with someone calling me an asshole."

Luke turned to the bloodied man lying on the floor then back to Dale. "You're fired! I don't care if you are my wife's husband! I won't have you working here."

Dale paused for a moment, then turned and stormed out of the building. He had been fired from other jobs in the past, but never had he tried so hard to be a good employee. He wanted to be successful simply because he was working for

Rachel's brother. Not only would it be shameful for him if he failed, it would be even more embarrassing for Rachel.

Dale walked aimlessly down the streets of the small town. He was fuming with anger and hoped that by spending some time walking down the sidewalks it would hopefully relieve him of the rage that he felt inside. Dale had always known that someday he was going to do something or commit some heinous crime if for no other reason than to relieve this compulsion he had for doing something grave and sinful. He had committed many crimes in his life and had paid the price for doing them. But these were mediocre and without lasting affect. What he wanted was to commit a crime that would leave a lifelong impact. He wasn't quite sure what that crime might be, but he had a pretty good idea.

Dale turned the corner and stopped in front of The Corner Bar. In spite of the rage he felt inside, he nearly smiled as he opened the door. It was dark inside as most bars were, but this one seemed even darker. He paused just inside to get a feel for the interior. As his eyes adjusted, he could see that there was nothing but empty tables. Obviously, not many people drink alcohol in the morning, but he thought there might be someone inside. As he thought about it, he was surprised that they were even open for business at such an hour. He stumbled across the floor to the back corner. He sat at a table with his back against the wall. Within moments, a voice blared across the room.

"What will you have?" shouted a loud voice.

"The cheapest beer you got," Dale shouted. "Bring me two of 'em while you're at it."

A big man with broad shoulders and bulging arms soon brought two bottles of beer to Dale's table. "Anything else?" he asked.

"Naw. That will do for now."

Dale gulped down his beer and set the bottle down on the table. His eyes had now adjusted to the darkness, and he slowly scanned the room. As he expected, the room was empty except for one lone figure sitting at a table on the other side of the bar. He slowly sipped his beer as he studied the figure. From the outline and hair style, it appeared to be a woman. As if on cue, the figure slowly stood up and started across the room and stopped in front of Dale's table.

"Mind if I sit down?" she asked with a sultry voice.

"Help yourself."

"You looked a bit lonely," she said.

"There have been worse things said about me," said Dale as he studied her face.

"You look like you lost your best friend," she said.

"Well, that would be hard to do," he said with a smirk. "Since I don't have a best friend."

"Oh, that can't be true," she said. "Everyone has a best friend."

"Lady, I don't even have one friend...never did and probably never will."

She pointed at the extra bottle of beer. "May I?"

"Help yourself," said Dale then turned to the bartender who was already walking towards their table with two new bottles.

"Why haven't you ever had any friends?"

"I don't know," said Dale staring at the bottle in his hands. "Must be something about me. Can't blame it on others."

"Well, if you don't mind my saying so, you look a bit angry," she said sipping her beer. "Would you say that is a good description of the real you?"

"Some people might say that."

"Well, what about you? What do you think?"

"Hey, look, lady. I just got fired from my job just minutes ago. Who wouldn't be a bit pissed off?"

"Oh, sorry," she said. "What kind of job was it?"

"Mechanic."

"Did you work for Luke?"

"That was me."

"I heard a lot of good things about you," she said. "They say you are one hell of a mechanic."

"I guess not good enough."

"What happened, if you don't mind my asking?"

"Ah, just a little dispute," said Dale.

"You're name is Dale, isn't it?"

"Yeah. How did you know?"

"It's a small town," she said with a smirk. "Everyone knows everybody and everything that's going on."

"What's your name?" Dale asked.

"Grace," she replied.

"Grace? Sounds religious. You ain't some kind of nun or something, are you?"

"Not hardly. In fact, anything but that."

Dale smiled. "Sounds like my kind of woman."

Grace paused as she stared at Dale. "You know, I'm a pretty good judge of character, and I definitely see something different about you."

"What d'ya see?"

"You ain't gonna like what I see in you."

"What a shock," said Dale. "Tell me anyhow."

"Well...I see a very hostile man, one who is capable of committing serious crimes."

"Really? Why would you say that?"

"I knew a man a long time ago," she said. "In fact, he was a friend of mine. He was almost a carbon copy of you. He always seemed so hostile, like he wanted to do damage to someone or something. It was if he was mad at life all the time."

"What happened to him?"

"He, unfortunately, brutally murdered his mother. It seems that he had a terrible childhood, and she was the cause of it. I guess she would never leave him alone. She would even cause him pain once in a while. By the way, how was your childhood?"

"I don't want to talk about it," snapped Dale.

"Oh! Did I hit a nerve?"

"Call it what you want," said Dale. "I just don't want to talk about my fuckin' mother."

"Wow! Okay. I guess we can find something else to talk about. Just tell me one thing. Do you consider yourself a hostile person? Are you like my long ago friend? Do you ever think about killing someone?"

"You sure ask a lot of questions."

"I promise I won't ask anymore," she said as she leaned over the table in Dale's direction. "I just want to know this one thing."

Dale paused as he gulped down his beer. "Yeah... I would say that I'm hostile. I could blame my mother, but I won't. She was mean to me...yeah, she was really mean to me, but I'm a grown up now. I know right from wrong. I can't blame her for everything that goes wrong. I can't blame her when I do something wrong. That's just plain stupid to blame others for what you do."

"Well, tell me," said Grace. "Do you think you could kill someone?"

"You don't give up, do you?"

"Just curious."

"To answer your question...yes, I could kill someone. I could kill someone and get great pleasure from it. I don't know why. I've been like this my whole life. I keep asking myself why would a normal person even consider such an act of violence then it dawns on me. I'm not a normal person. I don't think I have ever been normal. Makes you wonder, doesn't it? Why me? Why am I like this? I think about it everyday. I try to turn in another direction when these thoughts come to me, but I can't stop them. I saw a woman the other day walking down the street. I watched her for the longest time. I stared at her and imagined shooting her right in the head. Hell, to be more specific, I imagined shooting her in the ear. Now, when I look back at what I was thinking, I realize how sick that was. How could anyone stare at some innocent woman walking along and imagine shooting them? I say that now, but in no time at all I will be doing it again."

Grace leaned back in her chair. "Does this feeling come along very often?"

"It doesn't go away," said Dale staring at his folded hands. "And the worst part is everyday I get a little bit closer. I don't know when it's going to happen and I don't know for how long, but do know that there is a day that is coming that everyone will know who Dale Marlowe is."

Grace dropped her hands to her sides. "Wow! I can't believe I'm still sitting here."

"I can't believe I told you all that," said Dale. "I've never told a soul what you just heard."

"Don't worry," she said with a smile. "It's all safe with me."

Dale leaned back in his chair. "Enough about me. Who or, better yet, what are you?"

Grace smiled. "I'm just a girl...trying to make a living."

"Sitting in a bar?"

"Well...yeah."

"You're a whore, aren't you?"

"I'd rather not use that word," she said still smiling. "I like to think that I provide a service."

"Sitting in here?"

Grace turned and pointed at a door at the back of the room. "Wanna go see where I work?"

"Let's go," said Dale getting up from his chair.

It was an old door that seemed to blend with the walls around it. Grace opened it and let Dale inside. It was a small room with only a bed and a small refrigerator.

"I need fifty bucks," she said with her hand stretched out.

"Fifty dollars! I ain't never paid fifty dollars before."

"You ain't never had me before."

Dale dug into his pocket. "How 'bout twenty?"

"How 'bout getting the fuck out of here?"

Dale pulled out two twenty dollar bills. "That's all I've got."

Grace paused then snatched them out of his hand. She then walked over to the bed and sat on the edge. Dale followed and was soon sitting beside her.

He glanced at her chest. Her firm, ample breasts strained the buttons on her blouse. He slightly lowered his head to peek through the openings at the soft skin. He swirled his finger down her arm to the soft skin on the inside of her elbow. She was panting now. Her eyes were closed and sweat trickled down her neck and disappeared behind her blouse. He could see the outline of her hard nipples. His finger was only inches away. So far, it had all been innocent play. He had not crossed any line, but that was about to change. His head throbbed. He could feel the blood pounding through his veins.

Dale reached over and lightly touched the side of her breast. It was firm and yet soft to the touch. Grace jerked. She moaned and arched her back. Dale withdrew his finger. He wasn't sure. Was that a cold reaction? Was she pulling away? Then, she moved her chair closer and turned in his direction. "Please," she uttered softly.

Her breasts were right in front of him, heaving now from her heavy breathing. Dale could see her nipples through the sweat-soaked blouse. He could feel his manhood throbbing in his pants. He reached over and gently unbuttoned the top button of her blouse. He glanced at her face for a reaction.

"Faster," she muttered.

His hands trembled as he fumbled with the remaining buttons. When he finished with the last one, he slowly pulled her blouse open. Cool air from a slow-turning ceiling fan washed over her exposed breasts making her nipples even harder and leaving small bumps on her skin.

In spite of his gruff exterior, Dale knew women and he knew what pleased them. He reached over with both hands and lightly touched the sides of her bare breasts. She jumped slightly but moved even closer. He slowly moved his fingers to the underside of her breasts, caressing the soft skin, coming close to her nipples but never touching them. He then formed circles around the breasts even closer to her nipples, occasionally, brushing them as if by accident.

By then, her chest was rising and falling as she gasped for air. Dale firmly grasped her ribcage and leaned towards her. He lightly touched her lips with his. As she moved closer to kiss him, he pulled away, then, lightly hovered his lips over hers.

Crazed with lust, Grace pulled him close to her, savagely kissing his lips. The taunting and teasing was over. He wrapped his arms around her and kissed her long and hard. Still locked in a tight embrace, Grace slid her cotton blouse over her shoulders and let it fall to the floor. Dale fumbled with his belt sending his pants sliding down his legs. He stepped out of them just as she did hers.

"Take me now," she said with a raspy voice. "I don't care where, just do it."

Dale picked her up and sat her on the edge of the table. He grabbed her ankles and slid her closer to the edge. She fell back on the table. She wanted to scream. Her whole body was on fire. He had to do, and he had to do it now. What was he waiting on? She could feel hot liquid as it dripped from the tender folds of her skin and onto the floor. He wasn't going to tease her again. He wouldn't do that. He couldn't.

Then it happened. She felt his strong, hard manhood as it slid, effortlessly, into her. She screamed with pleasure. Her whole body screamed with pleasure. It was obvious that the teasing and taunting of foreplay was over. He was at the right height and could easily slam it deep into her. She screamed with pleasure at every thrust that he made.

Her first orgasm came within seconds, the second and third minutes later. He picked up speed, slamming home even faster. Grace was delirious with pleasure. Her orgasms seemed to be coming with every thrust. It went on for what seemed like an eternity. She had never experienced anything like this before. He was man enough. That was for sure. Just as she was about to pass out, he slowed his movement. He leaned his head back and emitted a guttural, almost primal growl. She felt him pulsating inside her, then slow to a stop.

"Good Lord, that was incredible," he said still holding her legs.

Grace ran her hands through her soaking wet hair. "I thought I was going to pass out."

He stepped back and helped her to a sitting position. "If there was anybody out there in the bar, I'm sure they thought from the way you were carrying on that someone was killing you."

She leaned on his shoulder. "Where did you learn all that?"

"What are you talking about?"

"Most men don't know the first thing about taking care of a woman," she said kissing his face and neck. "You had me on fire."

"One of my girlfriends used to tell me what felt good and what didn't," he said wiping the sweat from his face. "Ain't no secret to it. You just gotta tell us what ya like."

"You make it sound so easy."

"It is once a fella understands the plumbing of a woman," said Dale. He glanced at the clock on the wall then began putting his clothes back on.

"Gotta go?" she asked.

"Yeah."

"The old lady expecting you home by now?"

"Something like that."

"Anytime you want more of this, you know where to find me."

Dale opened the door and turned to Grace. "I'll keep that in mind," he said and walked out the door.

Five

It was early in the day, and it had just begun to snow. The weatherman had promised the snowstorm of the season with the possibility of ten inches of snow. The townspeople hustled to get ready by stocking up on food and drinks and checking to be sure that the snow blower was working.

Kramer knocked on his brother's front door. He waited for a few moments then tried again. Still nothing. He eased the door open and stepped inside.

"Erv," he shouted and from the kitchen he heard a slight groan. As he headed towards the kitchen, Kramer had a concern for what might be wrong with his brother, but he also had a good idea why he was groaning. As he walked through the doorway, his suspicions were confirmed. Erv was sitting with his head lying on the kitchen table in a pool of vomit and spilled vodka. Empty bottles were scattered across the floor.

"Jesus Christ, Erv! What the hell is your problem?"

Erv closed his open mouth, snorted and slowly leaned back in his chair. "What? Who's there?"

Kramer took a seat across the table from Erv. "What the hell are you doing?"

Erv slowly wiped his face with his shirt sleeve and stared across the table. "Not much of anything. What are you doing?"

"I'm staring at a God damn alcoholic."

"Oh, yeah? What's his name?"

"You know, I don't think this retirement thing is working all that great for you," said Kramer. "I thought you were going to do some painting and generally fix up the house."

"Yeah," said Erv. "That was the plan."

"What happened?"

"I don't know," said Erv. "I guess I came to my senses and realized how much more fun this is."

"You consider it fun when you have vomit on your face and down the front of you?"

Erv glanced down at his shirt. "Maybe I should wear a bib when I have a drink or two."

"I'd say you should be wearing a bucket around your neck when you're drinking," said Kramer. "I'd say you have a problem."

"Well, what the hell do you care?"

"Because you're my brother, and I care about you."

"You're beginning to sound more like a nagging sister."

Kramer took a deep breath and ran his hand through his hair. "You worked hard all your life, sometimes even putting your life on the line. You earned your retirement but not like this."

Erv slowly shook his head and then leaned forward onto the table. "I know you mean well, but I'm going to be okay. I know it doesn't look like it right this minute, but I'm going to do better."

"You've said that before."

"Well, I mean it this time."

"What's it going to take for that to happen?" Kramer asked.

"Hell, I don't know," said Erv. "I'm sure something will come along."

Kramer leaned back in his chair and glanced around the room. "Ever think about Dad? Remember what an incredible worker he was?"

"All the time," said Erv with a smile. "Hell, it was nine o'clock in the evening when he would finally sit down to read the paper."

"Now when I look back it amazes me how anyone could spend that much time working on a house," said Kramer. "He worked forty hours every week at the mill and just about that many hours improving the house."

"To him, that was pleasure. It was like a hobby for him. Personally, I look at it a little differently. I think of it as being a slave to your house. I've known people who are constantly working on their house. If they aren't doing some major project, they are cleaning or fixing something. In my book, that ain't fun."

"All I remember is watching Dad sitting down to read the paper and wondering if he would last for fifteen minutes before he would doze off," said Kramer.

Erv smiled as he remembered back. "By the way, have you heard from our sister again?"

"Not a word."

"She worries me."

Kramer got to his feet. "I got to be going. I have things to do."

"Me too," said Erv.

"Like what?"

"Oh, I don't know," Erv said with a smile. "Maybe I'll have a drink or two."

Kramer slowly shook his head and walked out of the room.

人 人 人

It was late afternoon when Dale opened the door of his house and walked inside. He glanced around the rooms looking for Rachel and finally realized that she must be visiting her parents. He imagined how they were most likely bad mouthing him. Wouldn't be a surprise. He grabbed a bottle of vodka and sat down in the living room. Might as well enjoy his private time while he could.

It was nearly two hours and a half bottle of alcohol before Rachel walked through the door. Dale was asleep in his chair, his head leaning back and his mouth wide open.

"Dale...Dale," she said with a loud voice. "Wake up."

Dale leaned forward and closed his mouth. "What?"

"What the hell are you doing?" she asked with an angry voice.

"Taking a nap. Why?"

"My brother called me," she said her voice growing louder.

"Yeah? And what did he have to say?"

"He said he had to fire you today," she said.

"Did he tell you why?"

"He said you were mean to a customer."

"Oh, he didn't tell you what the customer was like?"

"It doesn't matter. You don't treat customers like that."

Dale leaned forward in his chair. "Nobody treats me that way either. He's lucky I didn't kill the son-of-a-bitch."

"While all of this was going on, did it happen to occur to you that this is our only means of income? What little you make has been going for food and electricity. "

"Yeah, yeah, yeah," he said as gulped from his bottle of vodka.

"You don't get it, do you?"

"I will go out and find a job tomorrow."

Rachel slowly shook her head. "Why I ever married you I will never know," she muttered.

Dale slammed the bottle of vodka on the table and sat straight. "What did you say?"

"Nothing."

"Yes, you did. You said that you shouldn't have married me. Didn't you?"

"Oh, forget what I said. I didn't mean it."

"You didn't mean it? Then why did you say it?"

"I don't know," she said. "I said it out of frustration. I'm sorry."

There was a long pause. Dale leaned back in his chair. "I'm leaving first thing in the morning to look for a job."

"Okay."

"And by the way, I want you to dye your hair black," he said with no emotion in his voice.

"Are you kidding me? I'm a natural blond."

"I hate blonds," he said. "I'm asking you to please dye your hair."

"Let me guess...your mother was a blond."

"Never mind about that, just dye your hair."

人 人 人

It was the morning of January 14th. Dale was dressed and out the door even before Rachel had awakened. The bright morning sunlight brought the promise of a new day. Dale got into his car and was down the road in an unpredictable direction. He had no idea where he was going, but he knew that somehow he needed to vent this incredible rage he felt deep inside. He wasn't even sure why he had this constant anger. It seemed to have dominated his life as far back as he could remember. He knew that his mother's influence had much to do with it, but she wasn't the only reason.

There had to be other things in his past that had a negative influence on him. What was it? Why did he hate life so much? His childhood was not the best. There were things that happened back then. What were they? He had no friends when he was a child. That was for sure. Why was that? What did he do to alienate himself from the others? What was it?

"Eyes of the devil," said Dale aloud as he turned onto a road that would take him out of town. "If I had the eyes of the devil, why did you treat me like that? Why weren't you afraid that I would hurt you if I had the eyes of the devil? I should have. I should have hurt you...all of you. I can't believe I took your abuse and did nothing about it. Especially you, Megan. How could anyone be so cruel? My God, how did I live this many years since that day and not remember it 'til this moment? You were such a bitch. I should have paid you back somehow. You asked me to take you to the prom then convinced me that everyone would be wearing jeans and tee shirts. They all laughed at me. Everyone laughed at me. If they weren't there, they found out about it and ridiculed me later.

You should have paid for that. Hope you are proud of yourself. The only blond in school and you did that to me."

Dale pulled over and parked at the side of the road. He reached into the back seat and pulled out a bottle of vodka. He unscrewed the cap and upended it. It just seemed like it was one thing after another when he was a kid growing up. Probably the thing that started it all was when he failed the second grade. If that wasn't humiliating enough, the teacher had to announce his failure to the class.

"Why did you have to do that, Mrs. Dunson?" Dale muttered aloud as he gulped more vodka. "That wasn't fair. Do you know what that did to me? Everyone hated me after that. Everyone made fun of me. You shouldn't have done that. Jon Miller failed the second grade as well. You didn't announce his failure to the entire class. I just don't understand. You need to apologize to me. You, like so many people, owe me an apology. I want an apology right now, and I'm going to get it."

Dale gulped nearly the entire bottle of vodka and threw the empty onto the floor of the car. He put the car in gear and took off down the road. His mind was elsewhere not really knowing or caring where he was going.

Hours passed, and Dale found himself driving down a four lane highway with a sign that said Cincinnati was only a few miles ahead. He had been in Cincinnati many times before but usually on business. He was not by any means familiar with the city, so to avoid confusion; he took an exit off the highway, and soon found himself in a business section of town. He made several random turns and found himself in the parking lot of a mall called Eastgate.

Dale walked the aisles and hallways occasionally glancing at storefronts but not having any real interest. Rather, he spent most of his time watching and monitoring the passing of young women. After taking a seat on a stone bench and staring at the increasing number of beautiful women, his raging anger turned to lust. Within a short time, he found himself trying to judge the women's characters simply by their looks as they passed by. Most of them were young women at or near his age some with young children, others alone. He was amazed and surprised by the number of beautiful women passing by. He had never spent much time in shopping malls. He had never found much interest, and there were not that many near where he lived.

He couldn't help but wonder how many were here for important reasons and how many just to browse. He had heard it said that many women spend their time in shopping centers searching for a man. With that in mind, he centered his search for just such a woman. He was convinced that the majority of the women passing in front of him had that as their objective. If that were the case then why were they not looking at him? There were dozens every minute walking by him, and not one of them even glanced his way. He knew that he wasn't the most handsome man in the world, but he wasn't the ugliest either. Was it him, or were these women too self-centered and sophisticated for such a man as himself?

Dale turned in time to see a woman in a dress and high heels walking in his direction. Her beauty was beyond words. He quickly glanced away. The sound of her heels against the hard floor grew louder as she came closer. She was the one. All of the others were much too busy to notice him. This one has him in her crosshairs. She will stop and ask him to take her to lunch. There's no doubt. The others will be jealous. They will be sorry they didn't stop. How could they have let him get away?

From the sound of her shoes, she was getting closer. Should he look up at her and smile, or should he play hard-to-get? Of course, he will have to look up at her when she stops in front of him. That's for certain. He couldn't continue to stare at the floor with a beautiful woman standing in front of him. There is no doubt that she will be smiling; one of those suggestive smiles, the kind that tells you she's available and all you have to do is smile back.

She was within a few feet of him now. Should he look now? Everyone around him had to have, at least, glanced at her. You couldn't help but hear her. She had to have found pleasure in people looking at her. That was obvious from the sound of her shoes. They screamed, "Look at me!" Of course, that fits most all women. Why would they wear such loud shoes? Why do they paint themselves with colors? There's nothing natural about a woman. Even their hair is fake.

It was time. Should he look up at her? Should he smile? Should he say something? Her steps were louder. There were her beautiful legs. They went up and down with such determination. They seemed to be going faster. For God's sakes woman, slow down. She will not be able to stop at that rate. It's time. It's time. It's time for her to stop right now.

Dale looked up just as she passed by. His smile disappeared. Where was she going? Why didn't she stop? The clopping of her shoes was now fading away; her hair bouncing with each step.

"That bitch!" Dale said aloud as he turned his stare back to the floor. "What did I do to her? She thinks her shit don't stink. They're all alike. She thinks she is so much better than me. I may not be perfect, but I don't have to paint my lips with red shit every morning. I don't have to paint them again after I eat something. I don't have to paint my eyes so that they look like pee holes in the snow. A bald man wears a wig, and women laugh at him. They look at each other and wonder why he can't just be natural. Huh? You have the nerve to say that?"

Dale glanced at the now fading footsteps. His anger turned to rage. "I should have killed her right there on the spot. I could have made it out of here. Everyone would have been so stunned. Security don't carry guns. I could have been gone before a cop would have got here. God damn women! Think their shit don't stink!"

⅄ ⅄ ⅄

Her name was Helen Thompson. She had been looking for a job ever since her divorce. It had been a short marriage and one without children which left her penniless and without any support from her ex-husband. With no money and no place to live, she was forced to move back with her mother. It wasn't the worse thing that had ever happened to her, but it was a bit humiliating. Once settled in, finding a job became a priority with Helen. She had no education other than high school, and she had no training in a specific line of work. The only job that she had ever held was cashier at a local grocery store.

After scouring her hometown for a job and finding nothing, Helen decided to try her luck in a city shopping center. It seemed logical to her. If her only job experience was working in a store, why not go to a place where there are dozens of stores? She had made several stops and had filled application forms, but nothing seemed all that promising. The usual response was, "If something comes up, we'll give you a call."

Helen walked out of the mall and headed for the parking lot. It was a cold day with dark clouds rolling ominously across the sky. She pulled up her collar and started searching for her car. It was her habit to park at the back of the lot. Too many times she had found her car door dented from discourteous people opening their doors far enough to slam into hers. Helen figured that the odds of that happening at the rear of the lot where her car is usually by itself were practically nil. She could hear someone following her but thought nothing about it.

Upon reaching her vehicle, she pulled her keys from her purse. As she poked the key into the lock, she heard a voice, "Unlock this door."

She looked up to see Dale staring at her from the other side of the car. He pointed a revolver at her. "Now!" he said.

She opened her door and hit a button that unlocked the passenger side, and Dale got inside the car. She slid inside and closed her door. "What do you want?"

"Start the engine, and let's get out of here," he said still pointing the gun at her.

"Please don't shoot me! I'll do anything you want me to!"

"Come on," said Dale. "Let's get out of here."

Helen drove out of the parking lot and was soon on a road that would take them out of town. She was deathly frightened, but, in her mind, she was convinced that if she did what she was told, she had a chance to survive the ordeal. Defying him or putting up a fight offered no chance at all.

"Do we know each other?" she asked.

"No," he replied.

"Would you mind telling me what this is all about?"

"Back there in the mall...why did you snub me like that?" Dale asked with an angry voice.

"What are you talking about?"

"You walked right by me," he said his voice getting louder. You didn't say a word. You didn't smile. You didn't even look my way."

"I still don't know what you're talking about. Where were you?"

"I was sitting on a bench, and you walked right by me."

"What bench? I didn't see you."

"You were struttin' your stuff, weren't ya? I saw ya go by. You were asking for it, weren't ya?"

Helen turned and stared at Dale in disbelief. "What in God's name are you talking about?"

"Don't play that innocent game with me," said Dale. "I know your kind. You act like some kind of whore, then when it comes down to push or shove, you walk away. You get off teasing men. Let 'em think they're going to get some then you cut 'em off. I've seen your kind before."

"Okay. Let me explain it to you," she said with a calmer voice. "I lost my job back in my hometown, and I came here trying to find a new one. The last guy I talked to was being a real jerk. I was mad. I was upset. I just wanted to get out of there."

"So, you took it out on me, huh?"

"What are you talking about?"

"You strutted your stuff in front of me trying to turn me on," said Dale.

"No, I didn't! I didn't even see you there."

"Yes, you did. You walked right by me. You're not blind."

"I had other things on my mind," she said her voice now shaking.

"Yeah, I know what you had on your mind, little lady. You wanted to flaunt that stuff in front of me. Bet you'd like to have some of this, but you ain't gettin' it. That's what you were thinking, wasn't it?"

"No, I'm telling you the truth. I didn't have anything like that in mind," she said with tears falling down her face. "I've been desperately trying to find a job and have had no luck."

"Why don't you become a whore? You certainly dress like one."

"Please don't shoot me," she said as she broke down in tears. "I'll do anything you want if you will just let me live."

"Turn down that road right there," said Dale pointing at the side road.

Helen turned off the main highway and lowered her speed. "Where are we going?"

"I'll tell you when we get there, so just keep driving," said Dale.

"I'm so scared," she said as she broke down in tears. "I pray to God..."

"God ain't gonna help ya. Just like everyone else, you're on your own," said Dale. He paused as he studied Helen's head. "Are you a real blond?"

"No," she said. "I dye it blond."

"Why?"

"Why do I dye it?"

"Yeah. Why do you dye your hair?"

"I don't know," she said with a look of surprise. "I guess because it's the fashion. Everyone likes blonds."

"I don't."

"Oh...sorry."

"What is the real color of your hair?"

"I'm a brunette."

"Why didn't you just say that your hair is naturally black? Why do you have to call it brunette?"

"I don't know. I guess it's just the way women refer to their hair."

"Women," muttered Dale as he slowly shook his head. "Women have some strange ways of thinking."

Helen wiped her eyes with one hand. "What do you mean?"

"It's pretty much a given that whatever Muffy is doing you will all follow suit. If the style is to wear a burlap sack, you all would do it. Am I not right?"

"Well, whatever is in style is..."

"That's what I'm talking about," said Dale with a loud voice. "You don't have any brains to think on your own. You have no independence! I can understand teenage girls trying to keep up with the others but not grown women. Why can't you think for yourself?"

"I don't know," she said cautiously. "I do on many things. I just don't..."

"Do you have any kids?" he asked.

"No."

"Did your parents ever drag you by the ear?"

"Huh?"

"Never mind," said Dale as he pointed to a barn sitting by itself in an empty field. "Pull over there in front of that barn."

Helen began to cry aloud. Her hands were shaking uncontrollably on the steering wheel. They both got out of the car and started for the barn door.

"Please don't hurt me," she said as he closed the door behind them.

"Get down on the ground next to that bale of hay," he barked.

As she carefully sat down on the hay-covered floor, Dale walked over and grabbed a piece of rope. "Put your arms behind yourself and around that bale of hay," he said getting down on his knees. He grabbed her hands and tied them together.

Helen began to scream hysterically.

"Shut up, bitch!" Dale shouted as he pointed his gun at her.

"Please! Please don't do this!"

Sudden anger swept across Dale. He thought about killing her outright, but he really wanted her alive for the next few minutes. He glanced around the barn until he saw a tool box. He rummaged through it until he found a roll of duct tape, tore off a piece and turned back to Helen. By then, her voice was a bit hoarse. Dale straddled her with his knees on the ground and forced her to close her mouth long enough for him to spread the tape over it. He then pulled back and stared at his captive smiling at the results and proud of what he had done.

Dale reached down and grabbed her legs. He then pulled her until she was lying flat on the ground. Her skirt was now pulled up revealing most of her legs. He reached around and unzipped her skirt and slowly pulled it off. He smiled as he stared at her soft legs and white panties.

Even though the duct tape was still in place, Helen's screaming was still ear shattering. She now began to flop her body from side-to-side and all over the ground. Anger once again flooded over Dale.

"Stop that!" he shouted.

Her defiant actions seemed to increase.

In a total outrage, Dale reached over and grabbed his revolver. He leaned over and stuck the open end of the barrel in her ear. The frantic woman froze. In desperation she tried desperately to peer at the cold barrel of the gun. Dale pulled the trigger. There was a loud report, and Helen went silent; her body at ease. Dale stared at the blood splattered over the hay covered floor. He tried to line up the direction of the bullet as it had left her skull to see where it had gone, but he could not find any holes in the wall of the barn.

Dale stared down at the lifeless body in front of him. A smile slowly spread across his face. He grabbed her panties and ripped them from her body. With both hands, he lifted her legs and spread them apart. He unzipped his pants and pulled out his now hard member. Within seconds, he had thrust it deep inside her lifeless body. Less than a minute later, he was done. He pulled it out and zipped up his pants as he got to his feet. He smiled as he stared at the lifeless body, turned and was out the door.

It was a long drive back to his home in Prospect. His biggest concern was not to have any confrontations with the law, so he was very careful not to exceed the speed limits. He drove slowly down back country roads trying at all costs not to encounter anyone that he knew and especially any police officers.

"It was your fault!" Dale shouted from the driver's seat. "I told you to shut your fucking mouth. You might still be alive if you had taken my advice. Naw, I take that back. You were going to die just the same. Hey, if you had kept your mouth shut, you could have at least enjoyed the sex. I know I did. Don't feel bad. You might be the first, but you ain't the last. There will be more...many more. I'm just gettin' started. I'm gonna kill as many of you bitches as I can. Did you hear me?"

It was late in the evening when Dale pulled in front of their house. By looking through the window, he could see Rachel sitting in front of the television.

"Turn on the news," said Dale as he entered the room.

"What did you say?" she asked.

"Turn on the news. I want to watch the news."

Rachel reached up and turned the channel. "Why? You never want to watch the news."

"Well, I do this time," he said with a gruff voice.

"Any luck?" she asked.

"With what?"

"Good Lord, Dale. You supposedly spent the entire day looking for a job. I was wondering if you had any luck."

"No. Not really. I'll try again tomorrow. Turn it over to channel seven. They always have the best news."

"Dale! What the hell is going on? You aren't in the news, are you?"

"Will you shut up for a minute, so I can watch the news?"

"Well, I've had enough of this shit," she said as she got to her feet. "I'm going to bed."

It was late the next morning when Dale left the house in search of a job. He got in his car and headed for the downtown area. Slowly, he cruised the stores looking for a Help Wanted sign in the window of any store. After several sweeps of the area, he found himself parking in front of The Corner Bar. He got out of his car and walked inside. As always, it was dark inside with the owner wiping a beer mug with a towel.

"Is Grace here?" Dale asked.

"Have a seat, and I'll get her," he replied.

Dale groped his way towards the back of the room and soon found the table he had sat at once before.

"Well, look who's back," she said carrying a tray of beer bottles over her head. She set it on the table in front of Dale.

"A woman after my own heart," Dale said as he grabbed a beer.

"I didn't expect to see you back here so soon," she said. "Horny already?"

Dale paused as he stared at his beer. "Just had to get away."

"You look a little down," she said with a seductive voice. "Wanna go back there again?"

"Is this some kind of a whorehouse?"

"No. Not really."

"Then, who's the guy at the bar?"

"That's my husband."

Dale paused. "Are you kidding me?"

"No. Why?"

"He had to have known that we went back there and knocked one off," said Dale with a forced grin.

"We have what one might call a token marriage. He does what he wants, and I do whatever I want to do. I know it sounds a bit freaky, but it works for us."

Dale paused then leaned closer. "I think of you as a pretty liberal thinker."

"I suppose you could say that."

"For the first time in my life, I need someone to talk to, and I really believe that whatever I would tell you would be kept between the two of us."

"Oh, I think you can depend on that," she said. "You sound pretty serious."

Dale grabbed his head with both hands. "Have you ever killed someone?"

"Wow! This is serious."

"Well?"

"Of course not," she said with a grin. "I've met some people over the years that have put me to the test." The smile left her face as she studied this man in front of her. "You have, haven't you?"

Dale leaned back and glared at her with a cold look. "Yes."

"Pretty recently I'd say."

"Yes to that question as well."

"I somehow get the feeling that you're not finished either," she said with certainty.

"It just seems that all my life I was destined for this. I'll admit that I have anger issues. I don't remember a time when I wasn't angry. Sometimes I show it, but most of the time I try my best to keep it hidden. As strange as it might seem, I want to go on a killing rampage. I want to kill as many people as I can. I want to go down in the books as a serial killer. I want to be remembered."

"I gotta tell ya," said Grace. "Most people want to be remembered for a lot better things than that. You have some real serious issues. What was your childhood like?"

Dale's lips tightened. "If you knew what that was like, you would understand my anger."

"You're serious about becoming a serial killer, aren't you?"

"Oh, I'm serious, alright."

"Are you keeping it all right here in Ohio, or are you branching out?"

Dale paused and gave her a puzzled look. "For some reason, I don't think you believe me."

"Oh, I believe you," she said. "Keep in mind that you're talking to a woman who has seen and done just about everything under the sun. There's nothing that you could say or do that would surprise me."

Dale smiled. "You are one hardcore woman."

"You haven't answered my question."

"What's that?"

"Are you only going to kill people here in Ohio?"

"I really have no plans," said Dale. "I would like to make it down to Florida. That state is full of old people just sucking up good air. They need to go."

"You don't like old people?"

"I don't like any people," he said with a determined voice. "I figure if I take out a few old people, I will be doing the world a service."

Grace leaned back. "How do you know I won't go to the police?"

"You wouldn't do that," said Dale with a smile. "I know your kind. Actually, I've never met anyone quite like you. I have never talked about myself like I do with you. Your husband has got one hell of a wife."

Grace jabbed her thumb over her shoulder. "Wanna slip back there again?"

Dale paused then jumped to his feet. "Sounds like a winner to me."

Six

It was nearly two in the afternoon when Erv heard a knocking on the door. He rolled out of bed and started for the door. The knocking began again, this time much louder. Erv hurriedly opened the door.

"Jesus Christ, Erv," said Kramer. "Are you just getting up?"

"Well, I was just getting..."

"Never mind that shit," said Kramer. "Sit down. I have some bad news." They both sat on the sofa. Kramer turned to face his brother. "Our sister, Helen...I really don't know how to say this, but she has been killed."

Erv sat straight with his eyes trained on his brother. "What?"

"It looks like she was murdered."

"What are you talking about?"

"They found her body in a barn near Cincinnati. She had been shot in the head."

"Oh, my God," said Erv as he leaned back in the sofa. "How do you know this happened?"

"I got a call from the Cincinnati police. They tried calling you, but your phone was unplugged."

"I can't believe it," said Erv in a daze. "Do they know who did it?"

"They have some evidence," said Kramer. "But they really need us up there. They know that you are an investigator so they are leaving things alone until we get there."

Erv paused for a moment then jumped to his feet. "Let's go."

It was a long and tense filled trip for the two men. Not much was said as they tried to imagine what it would be like to stare at the dead body of their only sister. There was always the slight hope that the information was reported incorrectly, and that the body that supposedly belonged to their sister actually belonged to someone else. Erv couldn't help but wonder what kind of evidence was left behind. In his past experiences with murder cases, normally, there was no evidence left behind. The only type of murder that Erv had found evidence was when anger between two people resulted in one killing another. Such a murder involved no planning and very little removal of evidence in the aftermath.

It had seemed that they had taken forever to make the trip, but they were soon turning down the country road that led to the barn where their sister had been killed. Kramer was driving, and his hands nearly shook from fear as he turned off the road and parked in front of the barn. They knew that they had found the right place because of the police tape across the door and a police car parked near the barn.

Kramer slowly turned to Erv. "I'm scared," he muttered.

"I am too," said Erv.

"What the hell are you scared about?" Kramer asked. "You've been doing this nearly all your life."

Erv turned to his brother. "Kramer," he said with a stern voice. "This is our sister we're talking about. I'm going to try to do this by the book and all the while my heart is breaking."

Kramer paused. "Sorry," he muttered.

"Come on," said Erv opening the car door. "Let's go see what happened."

As they approached the barn door, a uniformed officer stepped out and held up a hand. "You can't come in here," he said with a harsh and stern voice. "There is an investigation going on here."

Erv pulled out his badge and flashed it at the man. "We'll only be a few minutes," he said. "Do you mind?"

The officer paused for a moment then stepped aside. "Only a few minutes and don't touch anything."

"Thank you, officer," said Erv as they walked inside the barn.

Kramer leaned over next to Erv and whispered, "Why didn't you tell him that the woman inside is our sister?"

"He wouldn't have let us in," said Erv with a soft voice. "Cops don't let relatives of murder victims investigate."

"Why not?"

"Too much emotion. You can't do an objective investigation. Trust me. I've seen it all."

Kramer turned to look at the hay-covered ground in front of him. Erv started to tell him something else but was shocked at the look he saw on his brother's face. He turned his head in the direction that Kramer was facing.

"Oh, my God," Erv muttered.

Kramer fell to his knees and stared helplessly at the blood-soaked hay. "I cannot believe this. Look at all of the blood!"

"I've seen this kind of thing a million times," muttered Erv, "but it has never been someone I knew and certainly not a relative."

Kramer wiped tears from his eyes. "Is it normal to see this much blood?"

"He shot her in the head."

"How can you tell?"

"There's a piece of her skull over there."

Kramer turned to see where he was pointing. There, lying on the soft layer of hay, was a piece of bone about the size of a quarter. It almost seemed to shine as it lay there almost floating in a puddle of blood. Kramer slowly got to his feet. Hiding his face with his outstretched hand, he walked slowly to the barn door.

"I can't take this," he said.

Erv walked over and wrapped his arm around his brother. "Maybe you should go some place while I check this out."

"I'll be alright."

"Are you sure?"

"Yeah," Kramer waving his hand. "Go do what you have to do."

Erv turned and studied the area. He knew in the back of his mind that for his brother's benefit, he had to make his investigation as quickly as possible. Actually, there wasn't much to see and very little evidence remained. Obviously, Helen had been held down by a strong man. The hay was evenly distributed with no piles or bare spots. If it had been anybody other than a strong man, there would have been signs of her flailing her arms and legs.

"Somebody you know?" asked the officer.

Erv turned to the uniformed officer standing behind him. "Just somebody from our hometown."

The officer turned to Kramer who was still wiping tears from his eyes. "Somebody you knew?" he asked.

"Don't pay any attention to him," said Erv with a loud and interruptive voice. "He ain't never seen this kind of thing before."

"Well, then, it's a damn good thing he didn't see the body," said the officer. "The head was damn near blown off."

Kramer slowly walked out the door heading for their car.

"She'd been raped too. What kind of guy would shoot a woman in the head and then rape the shit out of her? Just don't figure."

Erv gritted his teeth. "How did you know she had been raped?"

"Well, her panties were lying over there, and her dress was pulled way up. I ain't no genius, but that there is a sure fired bet. Besides, there was...you know...goo dripping out of her."

Erv lost it. "Son-of-a-bitch," he blurted.

The officer paused as he stared at Erv. "Something tells me you know this woman."

"She's my sister," he muttered as he headed for the door.

"Hey, you ain't supposed to..."

"Too late now," he said as he left the building.

It was late in the evening when Rachel came home from spending some time with her parents. The lights were on in the kitchen, and there was an empty bottle of booze on the table. She walked into the living room to find Dale passed out on the sofa.

"Dale!" she shouted.

"Huh?" was his answer without moving.

"Dale, what the hell is wrong with you?"

He grabbed his forehead with one hand and sat up on the couch. "What the hell is your problem?"

"What is my problem?" she shouted. "My problem is you. I didn't know I was marrying an alcoholic."

"And that's a problem?"

"Look at you! You're a mess! There isn't a night that goes by that you aren't drunk! You have a problem."

"Yeah, I got a problem," said Dale with a touch of anger in his voice. "And that problem is you."

"Oh, good Lord, Dale. Look at you. You are pathetic. You have no job and no money, and yet you manage to buy gallons of booze. How do you explain that?"

Dale paused for a moment. His head weaved slightly back and forth. He then reached down and picked up a half empty bottle of rum. "Oh, yeah. I forgot about you," he said as he chugged it down."

Rachel stared at him for a moment then waved her hand in disgust. "I've had it with you. I'm going to bed," she said then stormed out of the room.

It was late morning when Rachel awoke from her night's sleep. She quickly rolled over and stuck out her arm to find no one there. That was no surprise. Nearly half the nights, Dale is either gone or lying drunk somewhere in the house. Early in their relationship, Rachel had an idea that drinking was a problem with Dale, but she simply dismissed it as a small problem that could be corrected.

Dale was aware that he drank on a regular basis, but he never considered it to be a real problem. He simply considered it something he did for entertainment. He enjoyed watching television in the evenings and drinking a tall rum and coke or two. He never considered it to be an alcoholic gesture rather an adult way of having fun.

However, as the years passed, the amount of alcohol that he consumed in any given evening increased at an alarming rate. In the beginning, he only drank small amounts mixed with soft drinks. He would get just a slight tingling feeling of intoxication. As the years passed, his drinks became void of any soft drinks at all. He found himself drinking entire bottles of alcohol, and, in spite of his addiction, he simply dismissed it as a part of his evening entertainment.

Rachel got out of bed and walked into the living room. Dale was sitting in the sofa staring blankly at the wall in front of him. He had a serious almost menacing look on his face. Rachel's anger subsided somewhat as she studied the foreboding look on Dale's face.

"Well, did you get enough to drink last night?" she asked as she sat next to him.

Dale said nothing. He didn't even flinch.

"You know sometimes I wonder about you," she said. "You aren't the wonderful guy I married. That's for sure. Look at you. You can't hold a job. You spend all our money on booze. If it weren't for my family, we would have no place to live. Did you know that my father is now paying for our electricity? Did you know that? How much lower can we get? Do you not have any pride at all?"

There was a long pause, then Dale muttered without moving, "Ever think about killing someone?"

Rachel jumped. "What?"

Dale slowly shook his head. "Nothing," he muttered.

"Did you ask me if I ever thought about killing someone?"

Dale turned to her. "Well?"

"No, I never have thought about killing someone! What is wrong with you?"

"Just thought I'd ask."

"Have you thought about killing someone?" she asked.

"Sure, I have, and I'll bet just about every normal person has thought about it."

"Normal people don't think about killing other people," she shouted. "But then again you ain't normal."

"Doesn't your father keep all his money there in his house?"

Rachel turned to face Dale. "Why did you ask that question?"

"I don't know. Just asked."

"You scare me," she said. "You really scare me. Normal people don't talk like that. It's my father, isn't it? You don't like my father, do you?"

"Not really."

"Why? What did my father ever do to you?"

"You don't remember, do you?"

"What are you talking about?"

"It was Christmas day, and we were invited over to your parents' house," said Dale with a touch of anger in his voice. I walked into the house and was told to remove my hat, and it wasn't a please or a thank you."

"And that's why you don't like him?"

"Is that any way to treat a guest in your house?"

"Well, it's not like he called you bad names," she said. "Besides...get over it. Carrying a grudge like that is something a kid would do."

"It's just the way he did it," said Dale easing back in the sofa. "Didn't appreciate that one bit."

Rachel paused then said in a quiet voice, "You scare me sometimes."

Dale leaned forward. "Didn't you tell me once that your father doesn't have a bank account?"

"Yeah. So?"

"What does he do with his money?"

"What do you care?"

"Just curious," said Dale.

"All I know is there is a safe somewhere in the house. I suppose he keeps his money in it."

Dale leaned back and said nothing.

Rachel got to her feet. "Sometimes I actually wonder who you are," she said as she stormed out of the room.

"Sometimes, I do too," muttered Dale.

入 入 入

"We got to get this guy," said Erv as he poured himself a drink. "Want one?"

Kramer paused. "Yeah. Why not?"

"If it's the last thing I ever do, I'm going to get this guy," said Erv as he handed a drink to his brother.

"Well, you're the retired cop," said Kramer. "What do we do now?"

"I'm going to check with whoever is investigating this crime, and then I'm going to contact some people I know. You see, more than likely, anyone who commits such a crime has done something like this in the past and got caught. I know someone who can check the records to find such a guy."

"Well, this is one time I'm glad you were a cop," said Kramer sipping his drink.

"I didn't get shit for a pay check, but there were some perks," said Erv. "Are you with me on this?"

"I need to make a few phone calls, and I'll be free to tag along. I don't know how much help I'll be, but I'll be there for you."

"I still can't believe this has happened to our sister," said Erv as he sat down next to his brother. "She was the kindest most generous girl I ever knew."

"You know, I told her that I would never tell you this, but I guess it's okay now," said Kramer. "Remember back when we were kids, and you wanted a telescope? You wanted one big enough to look at the stars. You wanted one so bad, but we couldn't afford to buy one. They cost more than even Dad could afford. Actually, I never did understand why you wanted one. You never did have such an interest. I always figured that you just wanted to point it at Peggy Johnson's bedroom window. That I could understand. Whatever the reason, our sister took it upon herself to earn the money to buy you the telescope that you got for Christmas."

"Wait a minute," said Erv. "Mom told me that she bought the telescope for me."

"That's the way Helen wanted it to be," said Kramer. "But she actually earned the money."

"Why didn't she take the credit?"

"She never said, but I think she knew that Mom and Dad couldn't afford it, and that's why she did it."

Erv paused as he thought about what was said. "Where on earth did she get that kind of money? That telescope had to have cost a hundred dollars, and back then that was an incredible amount of money."

"She got a job washing dishes at the Malbar restaurant downtown," said Kramer. "I don't know how long she worked there...maybe two months or more. I know that she worked hard and spent all of the money she earned on that telescope. She was quite a sister."

They both grew quiet. Erv slowly turned to Kramer. "We have to get this son-of-a-bitch."

"I'm with you a hundred per cent," said Kramer.

Seven

It was January 21st. It was an extremely cold day, the kind of day where people would declare that it was too cold to snow. In spite of that, a light snow began to fall. Dale opened his eyes and found himself alone in the bed. At first, it startled him somewhat to not find Rachel lying beside him, but the morning light from the bedroom window convinced him that he must have overslept. With any luck, he will soon find Rachel in the kitchen fixing breakfast.

Dale climbed out of bed with a smile on his face. That didn't happen all that often, mainly because it was usually the morning after a night of heavy drinking. Dale usually started his day with a headache and an upset stomach which almost always put him in a bad mood.

Today was different. Today, Dale walked into the kitchen with a smile and with hopes of helping Rachel fix breakfast. He knew very little about cooking but was anxious to set the table with plates and silverware. As he walked through the door, he found her rushing towards the backdoor. She had on dress clothes and a coat.

"Where are you going?" Dale asked with a bit of surprise in his voice.

"I'm going to apply for a job," she snapped.

"What kind of a job?" he asked.

"What difference does it make?" she asked as she opened the door. "Somebody needs to get one. We damn sure can't wait for you to do it."

Dale leaned forward to comment, but the door slammed shut as she left the house. He stormed towards the door but stopped as he peered out the window. She was already inside the car and pulling away.

"God damn that woman!" he shouted. He then began to storm around the house with clenched fists. "God damn her! She can't do that to me! Who does she think is?" Dale stopped and stared out the window at the house in the foreground. His clenched jaws loosened. "You're gonna pay," he said with a stern voice and a slight smile.

⅄ ⅄ ⅄

"Great breakfast," said George as he sat down on the couch with a fresh cup of coffee. Martha sat down across from him in her favorite easy chair.

"Well, thanks, George," she said as she sipped her coffee.

"I'll never get tired of eggs and bacon," he said.

"We should be eating something healthier than that," she said.

"Why? Wanna live forever?"

"Well, I'd kinda like to stick around for a few more years," Martha said with a smile.

The smile on George's face disappeared. "I just saw Rachel drive off. From the way she was driving I would guess that she was upset about something."

"Wouldn't surprise me being married to that Dale guy," she said. "I'd say it's just a matter of time before she comes to her senses and gets rid of him."

"You never did much care for him, did you?" George asked.

"I don't know," she muttered as if deep in thought. "There's something about him. I can't really put a finger on it. One thing is for sure and that is he has the eyes of the devil. He actually scares me when he stares at me."

"Well, I'll give you that one," said George. "He is a bit scary."

"I often wonder why Rachel married him," said Martha. "God knows she could have done much better than him."

"I think you know why she married him," said George with a slight grin.

"Why is that?" she asked with a quizzical look on her face.

"You know...the same reason we got married."

"Oh, go on with ya," said Martha as she dismissed his comment with the wave of her hand. "If you're talking about sex, that's not why we got married. We loved each other and still do. It wasn't about sex."

"Maybe not for you," said George with a broad grin.

"Oh, you men are all alike."

"Well, maybe in the beginning I was only interested in sex, but, unfortunately, I had to go and fall in love with you," said George. "Why couldn't I have just let well enough alone?"

There came a loud noise from the direction of the backdoor. It was the sound of someone stomping their feet as if they were trying to remove snow from their boots. The smile left George's face as he turned to see what was happening. It was obvious that someone was about to enter their house.

Suddenly, the door swung open. George leaned forward to see who it was. He felt a certain relief when he saw Billy standing there, holding an armload of logs and wiping his feet. George leaned back in his chair. Everything was okay.

Then, without warning, there came a loud report. Billy fell forward onto the floor, the logs scattering everywhere. George turned to see Dale step over Billy's body holding a gun at eye level. Dale turned the gun towards George and pulled the trigger. The bullet smashed into the side of George's head kicking him nearly out of his chair. He managed to crawl out of his chair but slumped onto the floor. Dale turned to Martha. By then, she was screaming at the top of her voice. He fired his gun at her. The bullet hit a cheekbone and exited through her forehead. Martha fell silent. Dale walked over, stuck the gun in her ear and pulled the trigger. The bullet tore its way through her skull shattering everything in its path.

Dale stepped back and scanned the room. There was blood and there were skull fragments everywhere. He paused as he studied the two corpses looking for signs of life. He snickered as he noticed that Martha was still holding her cup of coffee. He stuck his gun in his pocket and ran out of the house.

⅄ ⅄ ⅄

Erv combed his house with an empty trash bag picking up empty beer bottles as he moved from room to room. He then opened the refrigerator and removed the full ones as well. The bag was nearly full and heavy as he took it outside to discard into the trashcan.

"That sounds like empty beer bottles," said Kramer as he walked around the side of the house.

"They all aren't empty," said Erv.

"You threw away full bottles of beer?"

"Yep."

"Have you lost your mind?"

"Nope," said Erv closing the trashcan lid. "I lost a sister, and I'm going to do everything in my power to find out who did it and that includes giving up drinking...at least for a while."

Kramer paused. "Heard anything yet?"

"Gonna make some phone calls in a little bit," said Erv. "See if they have any leads yet. Come on inside."

The two men walked inside and sat down. There was a certain amount of tension in the air. Both men were suffering from the loss, but were uncertain as to the degree of sorrow the other one felt. Erv was convinced that he could revive his skills and experiences as a law enforcement officer and successfully find Rose's killer. Kramer, on the other hand, was at a loss as to what to do. He wanted to go someplace, do something that would help find this murderer. He knew that his lack of experience in the field of murder investigation put him in a situation where he needed to rely solely on his brother. All he could do was to be there for Erv no matter what he wanted. Kramer was reasonably certain that the two of them working together should be able to find this killer.

"So, what happens next?" Kramer asked.

"Well, I've made some phone calls, and I'm waiting for an answer," said Erv. "I maybe out of touch, but I still have friends in the business."

"What will they be able to tell you?"

"They are checking on anything happening recently that would be similar," said Erv. "Usually, when you get something like this, it ain't the first time for the guy."

"So, if they do call you and tell you there are other recent murders like this, what good does that do?"

"Well, the first thing I would do is try to tie the two murders together to determine if it is one guy. That's not all that hard to do. Every murderer leaves behind something unique."

"Okay, so then what? You're pretty sure he has committed two murders. What good is that for catching him?"

"You'd be surprised at what some small little quirk can lead to the killer," said Erv. "Besides, now you have two locations, one leading to the other. This usually sets a pattern as to the direction that he is going. Nearly all mass murderers follow one direction and very seldom change. Knowing which direction they are going isn't much help, but it's a start."

Kramer paused. "You know when the time comes that we have him in our custody, it's going to take everything I have to keep from killing the son-of-a-bitch."

"Well, there's no way we can..."

"Do you mean to tell me that if we had this animal out in the middle of nowhere, and he has confessed to killing our sister, you wouldn't want to shoot the bastard?"

"Oh, I didn't say that," said Erv. "I can't imagine how I will be able to keep from killing this guy."

Just then the phone rang. Erv picked it up and fell silent. The look on his face grew distraught; his color turned pale. Kramer could hear screaming coming from the phone but could not determine who it was. He moved closer with hopes of learning more about whatever was going on.

Suddenly, Erv jumped out of his chair and started for the door. "Let's go."

They were soon in Erv's vehicle and down the road. Kramer couldn't contain himself any longer.

"What's going on? Who was that on the phone?" he asked.

"Remember Rachel Armstrong, the lady who married some guy from out west?"

"Yeah."

"That was her on the phone. She was screaming hysterically. All I could pick up is that she just came home and found her family all dead. She said there is blood everywhere."

"Oh, my God!" muttered Kramer. "Why did she call you?"

"She's in a panic and doesn't know who else to call," said Erv. "She's totally out of her mind right now. Imagine coming home and finding such a thing."

"Well...what can we do?"

"We're going to conduct an investigation," said Erv. "Whatever you do don't touch a thing. As soon as I have gathered enough evidence, I'll make a phone call."

"Whoa!" said Kramer. "I wonder if this has any relationship to Rose's murder."

"Now, you're clicking," said Erv. "We never have such a thing as a murder around here, and all of a sudden there is a rash of them. Chances are real good that they are related."

"So, you're thinking that the guy who killed our sister had something to do with this?"

"Chances are real good," said Erv.

He pulled into the driveway and turned off the engine. They sat there staring at the house for several moments.

"Cannot believe how nervous I am," said Kramer.

"To tell you the truth, so am I," said Erv turning to his brother.

"Why on earth would you be nervous?" Kramer asked. "You did this for a living."

"I did wife-beatings and break-ins."

"You've never investigated a murder before?"

"Oh, yeah," said Erv. "But nothing like this."

Suddenly there came the sound of a woman crying from inside the house.

Erv turned to his brother. "Let's go."

By the time they reached the front door, it was already open. "Thank you for coming, Mr. Meyers," she said wiping the tears from her eyes. "I know you are retired and I shouldn't be bothering you, but I just didn't know what to do."

"That's quite alright, Rachel. I understand," said Erv.

The two men stepped inside and scanned the room. "Oh, my God," muttered Kramer. The blood had already dried on the walls, and yet pools of it remained on the carpet. The young boy was lying on top of three logs in such a manner that if it wasn't for the dried blood on his back, one would guess that he was asleep. George was curled up and lying on blood-soaked carpet.

Erv turned to Martha and was amazed at what he saw. She was sitting upright in her chair. There was a bullet hole in the side of her head and her forehead with blood covering her lower body, but the strangest thing that caught Erv's attention was the fact that she was still holding her coffee cup. He approached her very cautiously and peered into her cup to find it half full.

"Have you touched anything in here?" Erv asked.

"No," said Rachel. "At least, I don't think so."

Erv pulled a card from his wallet and handed it to her. "Here, call this number. It's Sheriff Jim Towle. He needs to be the one to investigate this crime."

Rachel took the card and reached for the phone.

"Not that phone!" Erv shouted. "There might be fingerprints on that one. Use another one."

Both men watched as she walked out of the room.

"You were getting rid of her, weren't you?" Kramer asked.

"It was that obvious?"

"Sure was."

"Well, I need a few minutes to examine these two and the room itself," said Erv as he searched the area around where Martha was sitting. "Besides, I really have no right to be here. I am retired and no longer an officer of the law."

"Could we get in trouble for being here?" Kramer asked.

"Not really. There is a professional courtesy among officers of the law. Besides, she called. Remember?"

Kramer paused as he watched his brother search the floor. "What are you doing?"

"Looking to see if he left anything behind."

Kramer began to search the floor as well. "What are we looking for?"

"Oh, an empty bullet shell, foot tracks in the blood, anything that looks like it doesn't belong."

Kramer's search took him to where Martha was sitting. He examined her blood-soaked head and glanced inside her coffee mug. "My God, have you ever seen anything like this?"

"Never."

"There is still coffee in her cup."

"I know. I already saw it."

"I don't know that much about this stuff, but wouldn't the blast from a gun in the head kick her in the opposite direction?" Kramer asked.

"You would think so, but it didn't seem to bother her."

"I still cannot believe it. If it wasn't for all of that blood, you'd swear she was still alive, sitting here drinking her coffee."

Erv dropped to his knees in front of the slumped body of George. He leaned over and pressed his ear against his open mouth to try to detect any breathing.

"Did you know George?"

"Not very well," said Kramer. "I'd see him in town every once in a while."

"Well, you won't be seeing him anymore."

"Dead?"

"Took a shot in the head just like she did," said Erv. "Whoever did this must have some kind of weirdo thing about shooting someone in the head."

"Well, I'm no expert, but I'd say that it usually does the trick."

Erv got to his feet and slowly examined the room. "This guy was pretty good. Didn't leave much behind."

"Is there anything else we can do?" Kramer asked.

"When Jim gets here, he will check for fingerprints and other stuff," said Erv. "I just don't think he's going to find anything."

"I called Sheriff Towle," said Rachel as she walked back into the room. He said that he would be here in a few minutes." She paused as she glanced around the room and then grabbed her face as the tears began to fall.

"Come on," said Erv leading her out of the room. "Let's go into the kitchen."

They all sat down at the table. There was a pause as Rachel regained her composure.

"I'd offer you some coffee, but there isn't any made," said Rachel wiping the tears from her eyes. "If you'd like some, I can have it ready in just a few minutes."

"No thanks," said Erv. "We're good."

"I am so sorry for calling you, Mister Meyers," she said. "I had heard that you had retired, but called you anyway. I just didn't know what to do, and I wasn't thinking too clearly at the time."

"That's perfectly okay," said Erv. "This retirement thing ain't working so great for me. Got too much time on my hands. Besides, I knew your parents very well, and I'd love to find the guy who did this."

"Is there anything I can do to help?" Rachel asked.

"I just need to ask you a few questions if you feel that you're up to it," said Erv.

"Go right ahead."

"Have you seen any strangers hanging around the house lately?"

"No...not really."

"Any friends or relatives visiting lately?"

Rachel thought for a moment. "There really haven't been any visitors lately that I've noticed."

"Had your mother or father had any confrontations or problems with someone in town?"

Rachel paused. "Well, not in town, but..."

"But what?"

"Well, my husband and my father have had their share of run-ins."

"Really? Where is your husband right now? I'd like to talk to him."

"Well, I'm wondering the same thing," she said with a look of concern. "I spent the day looking for a job, and when I got home he wasn't there."

"Any idea where he might have gone?" Erv asked.

"I have no idea," said Rachel. "We had a fight this morning. And that's the last I saw of him."

"Do you often have arguments with your husband?"

"We have been lately."

"Did he happen to mention your father this morning?"

"Yes, he did," said Rachel as she snapped her fingers. "He was asking me where my father kept his money. In fact, he was asking me all kinds of questions about my family. Now that I think about it, he was acting really strange."

"Didn't you say something about your husband and your father having some kind of arguments or confrontations?"

"Well believe it or not, my husband walked in that door right over there on Christmas day and didn't take his hat off," said Rachel. "Well, my father expects every man who enters his house to take off his hat. I'm sure it was some sort of a tradition back years ago. Anyways, he told Dale in a very abrupt manner to take his hat off. Well, Dale didn't appreciate that one bit, and he never got over it. I don't think that it was so much the fact that he had to remove his hat as opposed to how my father told him."

All of the time Rachel was talking, Erv was writing notes on a small pad of paper. He paused for a moment while he finished writing.

"Do you know where your husband was this past Tuesday?" Erv asked.

"Why?"

"Just curious."

Rachel glanced at the floor as she tried to remember. "Actually, he was gone the whole day looking for a job."

"Any idea where he went?"

"Well, he said something about going to Cincinnati," she said. "Didn't sound like it went very well. Why do you ask?"

Erv glanced at Kramer and then turned back to Rachel. "Our sister was murdered on that day a few miles out of Cincinnati."

Rachel's face sobered. Her hands went straight to her hips. "What's that suppose to mean?"

"Well, it doesn't mean a thing," said Erv. "We're just trying to gather the facts."

"What time of the day was she killed?" Rachel asked.

"Late afternoon... we're guessing," said Erv.

"That kinda fits," she muttered with a relaxed voice.

"What are you thinking?"

"He got home around six because the news had just started," she said. "He was acting really strange. He was anxious for me to turn on the news, and I don't think I ever saw him watch the news. I couldn't figure out why he was so excited about watching the news but now things are starting to come together."

"What are you saying?" Erv asked.

"I think there's a chance he killed your sister because I'm beginning to think there's a real good chance he did this," she said spreading out her hand.

"Now, Rachel," said Erv. "This could be an incredible coincidence. What makes you think that he did this?"

"He's a pretty strange fellow in the first place, and lately he has been a bit crazy," she said. "He gets drunk every night and talks crazy. I've never known anyone quite like him."

"What did you say his name is?" Erv asked still writing on his pad.

"Dale...Dale Marlowe."

"Anything else you want to tell me?"

"No...not that I can think of."

"I have to tell you that I'm a bit concerned for your safety," said Erv.

"Oh, I'll be alright," she said with a wave of her hand. "He won't hurt me."

"Are you sure?"

"Yeah...I'm sure."

"I have another question for you. Do you have any idea where he is heading?" Erv asked. "What state is he from?"

"Well, he was living in Wyoming when I met him," said Rachel. "But if he is a murderer, my guess is he is heading for Florida."

"Why do you say that?"

"More than once he has said how much he hates old people," she said. "For that reason he hates Florida because of all the old people down there. He even mentioned something about killing them all."

Erv turned to Kramer. "Let's go pack."

Eight

At the heart of Charleston, South Carolina on a back street surrounded by a neighborhood of older middle-income homes was a bar by the name of Cave Bar. It was an old building with antique furniture, dim lighting but an ample supply of alcohol. It had been a favorite of all the neighbors since its inception back in the early 1930's. Most of its regular patrons liked its relaxed atmosphere, but the most important asset of the Cave Bar was the close proximity. Nearly everybody was within walking distance, so if one ordered a few too many drinks, he needn't worry about getting home as long as he could still stand upright.

Dale opened the door and stepped inside. It was much darker than what he was expecting, so he stopped to allow his eyes to adjust. He soon found his way across the room to a table with four chairs nearly hidden in the back of the bar. He had just got seated when an older man stepped up to the table and set a frosted mug of beer in front of Dale.

"D'ya like beer?" he asked.

"Sure do," said Dale with a look of surprise.

"Well, you're new here, so the first one is on the house."

Dale leaned forward and grabbed the cold mug handle. "Thank you, sir," he said and gulped from the mug. "You can bring me another one in just a few minutes."

"Will do," said the man as he walked away.

Dale scanned the room as he set the mug onto the table. There were a few couples sitting at tables quietly discussing personal matter and the events of the day. Sitting on stools at the bar were older men who frequent the place on a regular basis. Their discussions of world events and the latest jokes were generally low key with an occasional outburst of laughter.

As Dale's eyes became more adjusted to the dimly lit room, he scanned the room one more time. There were four televisions mounted high on the walls. Nearly everyone in the room was either casting glances at one or more of them or did nothing but watch. The thing that had their attention was the broadcast of the Sunday night Super Bowl. The Cincinnati Bengals were struggling against the San Francisco 49ers. Since it is customary to root for the underdog, most everyone in the bar was a Bengal fan, and, as everyone expected, the Bengals were losing.

Dale leaned back in his chair and sipped his beer. He didn't remember that much about his father. He only lived with him for a short time. Watching football on television took him back to the good times when they would watch together. "We had fun watching football, didn't we Dad?" he muttered.

"We didn't have much in common, did we Dad? Football was one thing we both liked very much. The only other thing that I can remember was shooting guns. Remember Dad? Remember that Christmas...the only Christmas that we spent together, and you bought me a gun? "Dad, do you remember when I was a little kid, and you bought me a BB gun? Do you remember that, Pop?"

"God, I loved that gun," said Dale. "I was only about eight or nine years old as I recall and thought I was the toughest guy in the world now that I was the proud owner of a BB gun.

I remember that it was only a couple days after you gave me that gun that I was in back of the house shooting at just about anything in sight. I didn't know it at the time but you were watching me from a window when, suddenly, I began shooting at the birds sitting high up in the trees. I don't know whether I actually believed that I could hit one of them. They seemed so far off. Maybe, I thought of them as some kind of inanimate object. I don't know. All I know is that it wasn't long before I scored a direct hit, and to my surprise a bird began its descent from its perch, falling gracelessly as it bounced from one limb to another. I must say I was surprised. I never really thought that I would shoot one.

I remember that I walked over to the bird with a certain amount of apprehension. I wasn't sure if I should strut like some big game hunter after the kill, or cautiously creep up to the innocent little animal that I had needlessly destroyed.

I knelt beside the fallen bird, and with the end of my gun, I gently turned it over. From its pale red underside, I knew that it was a female robin. I remember wishing that it was only stunned, and that it would suddenly awaken and fly away, but that was not to be. Her head dangled, lifelessly, to one side, and a small trickle of blood oozed from under her feathers and dripped onto the ground.

I nudged the bird with my gun hoping to arouse it from some deep sleep. Nothing. By now, the tears were flowing from my eyes as I finally came to realize what I had done. A sweet and innocent life had been taken, and it was my fault.

I don't know how long you had been standing beside me, but, suddenly, you were there bending down on one knee. You stayed there for the longest time. I remember that. I was dying inside. I felt so bad. I had done something very bad and deserved to be punished, and you calmly stared at the dead bird.

Finally, you turned to me and asked me if I understood what had happened here. I muttered something about an accident and how I'd never do it again and then you told me something that I never forgot. In fact, I'm sure that was your intention that it would be a day that I would remember all my life. You told me that today was the day that the life of a small bird ended. Hardly seems significant in the big scheme of things, but nonetheless, we have one less bird in the world today. Tomorrow, there will be one less song being sung by a creature whose only goal in life is to give happiness.

You, then, laid a hand on my shoulder, and when I finally worked up the nerve to look you in the eye, I noticed a tear falling down your cheek. To this day, I can't remember another time that I ever saw you cry. You told me that since God loves all life, even the lowly robin, and there must be a reason for this seemingly senseless death. It was then that you told me something that would guide my life from then on. You told me that, without doubt, God sacrificed that little bird so that I would learn a valuable lesson. I would be a better person after having seen how precious life is. Life must be preserved at all cost. Then, you told me that I should always remember the lesson that I learned so that the robin's dying would not be in vain. Do you remember that, Dad?"

Dale paused. It suddenly occurred to him that he had been speaking aloud, and his voice had grown intense. He looked up and slowly scanned the room. Nearly everyone was staring at him. "Sorry," he said as he picked up his beer and drank from it.

Nearly an hour passed. The Super Bowl was in the fourth quarter, and the soon-to-be outcome was fairly obvious. Many of the patrons had gone home, while others were lost in conversation. Dale had just settled back in his chair when a young woman walked in. She was wearing a long flowing dress as she strutted across the room. Dale leaned forward to watch as she stopped at the bar. She was stunningly beautiful and had captured the interest of every man in the room including Dale. The bartender wasted no time taking her order. As she leaned back to wait for her drink, Dale got to his feet. He slowly walked across the room and plopped a five dollar bill on the counter beside the woman.

"Let me buy your first drink," he said.

She slowly turned and looked at the money then looked up at Dale with a forced grin. "I'm not the kind of girl you obviously think I am."

"And what kind of girl would that be?" he asked with a slight grin.

"I'm not a lady of the evening."

"Do you mean a whore?"

"That's another way of putting it."

"I was just sitting back there all alone, and you walked in," said Dale. "I could use the company. D'ya mind?"

She paused as she stared at his table then at him. "Why not? I came in here to watch the rest of the game."

"Did your TV go bad?"

"How did you guess?"

"Why else would you be here?" Dale asked.

"Maybe I wanted to meet someone like you."

Dale casually pointed at his table. "Well, this is my lucky day."

"What are you doing here?" she asked as she sat down at the table.

"Same as you," said Dale sitting down next to her. "Watching the game."

"Did your TV go bad as well?"

"I'm on a business run," said Dale. "Heading for Florida."

"And what kind of business are you in?"

"I...I fix cars, and they need me down there."

"They don't have anybody down there who knows how to fix cars?"

"It's...it's something special, and I am one of the few who knows what to do," said Dale. "Besides, it's the middle of winter, and I could use a little sunshine."

"What's your name?"

"Dale...Dale Marlowe. What's yours?"

"Lucy."

"Gotta last name?"

"Yeah."

"Well?"

"Be grateful I gave you the first name."

"Do I look that evil?"

She paused. "Do you really want an answer?"

Dale forced a smile. "I got a feeling that I'd be better off without it."

They both sipped their drinks then turned to watch the game.

"What kind of a job do you have?" Dale asked.

"I'm a secretary for a construction company," she said.

"Married?"

"Divorced."

"Aren't we all?"

"Why? Are you divorced as well?" she asked.

"Aren't we all?" said Dale with his hands out. "I don't think I know of any couple who has stayed married. What's that all about?"

Lucy sipped her drink. "I think it has to do with today's society and women in the work force. Back in the day, it was the man who earned the paycheck. The wife stayed at home to raise the kids and gab with the other women in the neighborhood. In today's workforce you have men and women working together, and I think we both know what that leads to."

"So…what should a couple do?" asked Dale. "They got bills to pay."

"That's just it," said Lucy. "People should run their family like a business. You have so much coming in and so much going out. In today's world, I don't think there is enough effort to consider those two figures. The amount coming in is pretty well fixed outside of a possible raise in pay once a year. It's the outgoing money that we can control but don't. The best example is transportation. Everyone in America thinks they must keep up with the Jones. If the Jones are driving a big expensive SUV, then everyone else has to. I read once that the average family pays out three to four hundred dollars each month for transportation. Good Lord, how much does that drain from the monthly budget?"

Dale smiled. "Might as well go by taxi. It would have to be cheaper."

"Remember when women stayed at home and fixed meals?" she asked. "Eighty per cent of the vehicles going through the drive through at McDonald's have one woman on board. That's how she feeds her family. Then, on a Friday night, they all go out to eat dinner at a restaurant and wonder why they have no money. It's crazy."

Dale leaned back in his chair. "You're quite a lady."

Lucy grinned with embarrassment. "I'll take that as a compliment."

"I've known a lot of women in my time, but I don't remember any particular woman who regarded life as a business. That's very commendable."

"I guess I've always been this way," she said taking another drink. "I've always been a dreamer, but realize that you must deal with life's problems in a realistic and factual way."

"You call yourself a dreamer," said Dale. "If you don't mind my asking, what do you dream about?"

"Oh, I've always dreamed about marrying the right person and having kids," she said with a sheepish smile. "I've always wanted kids."

"How many?"

"No more than three," she said with a warm smile. "Hell, at this point in my life, I'd settle for one. I guess I need to find the right man first."

"You were married at one time," said Dale, leaning forward. "What happened to that marriage?"

Lucy upended her drink and finished it. "You know, there's another thing about life that I have a problem with. Couples get married based on their experiences from dating someone. I think you should live together for a year or two before making that move."

"Well, that's one thing that I agree..."

"You can't base a relationship on what you ate at the restaurant or what movie you went to see. You need to experience day-to-day stuff like paying bills, washing underwear and mowing the grass. That's when you find the real person who is hiding behind that mask."

Dale smiled as he stared at her. "You're quite a lady," he said with a smile.

Lucy jumped. "Why do you say that?"

"I don't know. Not many women are that logical in their thinking," he said sipping his drink. "Most women think with their heart and soul. I'm not saying that's all that wrong. I'm just saying that I respect your way of thinking."

Lucy slammed her empty glass onto the table and scooted back her chair. "Got a place to stay for the night?" she asked with a smile.

"Come on," she said getting to her feet. "You can stay with me for the night. Only got one bed, but I'm sure we can make do."

"I'm right behind you," said Dale.

人 人 人

Erv pulled his car off the state highway and headed into a rest stop. He parked in front of a small building that housed restrooms, vending machines and telephones.

"Thank God," said Kramer. "I gotta get out of this car and take a walk."

"Yeah...me too," said Erv opening the car door.

"Why are we stopping?" Kramer asked.

"I gotta make a phone call," said Erv stretching out his arms. "I want to see if our Mr. Marlowe has been active again."

Erv picked up a public telephone while Kramer took a short walk. Within minutes, Erv hung up the phone and charged after his brother.

"Well, he's been at it again," said Erv.

"What happened?"

"It would appear that he has killed another woman, and she's only a few miles from here."

"I suppose the local police have already hauled her away," said Kramer.

"That's the best part of the whole thing," said Erv with a smile. "That friend of mine has set it up so that everyone thinks we are some secret agents for the government. They are leaving everything alone until we get there."

Kramer paused. "Doesn't that mean that we should get going?"

Erv turned to the car. "Let's go."

⅄ ⅄ ⅄

Lucy had lived on the third floor of a small apartment building. It was an old and tattered building on the poorer side of town. Erv slowly eased his car among the other six police cars that were already parked there. They both gazed the surroundings then got out of the car.

"They've waited all this time for us?" Kramer asked.

"Damn straight," said Erv. "Don't forget. We're top secret investigators. I think only the president and God can tell us what to do."

"What should we do?" Kramer asked. "I don't want them to get the impression that we are not what they think we are."

"Just stay quiet and follow my lead," said Erv. "We are going to search for any evidence to prove that Dale Marlowe was there."

"You must be Erv Meyers," said a uniformed officer with his hand out.

"That would be me," said Erv taking the man's hand.

"We haven't touched a thing. My instructions were very clear, so everything is just how we found it."

The two men stepped further inside and scanned the room. It was a small living room with only the essentials such as a small couch, and easy chair and a dining table with only two chairs.

"Where is the body?" Erv asked.

"In the bedroom," said the officer as he walked across the room. He stopped and pointed at a doorway. "She's in there lying on her bed. Looks like the guy did her before he shot her in the head."

Erv studied the body lying on the bed. "Why do you say that? She looks like she's fully dressed and I've never seen it where a guy puts her clothes back on."

"He had us fooled until we noticed one thing."

"What's that?"

"Her pants are on backwards."

Erv paused. "What?"

"One of the officers noticed it, and sure enough, the zipper is on her butt."

Erv and Kramer walked into the small bedroom and stopped at the side of the bed. She was a young and beautiful woman with long blond hair and a perfect body. She was lying with her head straight up with her still open eyes staring at the ceiling. There was a small trickle of dried blood that had dripped from one of her ears. On the other side of her head there was a massive hole where her ear once was. Chunks of bone and flesh were scattered over a dried pool of blood. There was a relaxed almost serene look on her face. It was as if she had just awakened from a long night's sleep.

Erv glanced down at the pants to verify that they were on backwards. He scanned the body to determine if anything else had been done to her. It was fairly obvious that she had had sex with a man, and that he had shot her in the head when he had finished. The only positive thing about the entire incident was that she had to have died instantly. Even her face had a distinct look of happiness and contentment.

"Well, one thing is for sure," said Erv. "It's fairly obvious that this is the work of Dale Marlowe."

"How do you figure?" Kramer asked.

"He had sex with his victim and then shot her in the ear, and this is the second victim. The act of shooting a woman in the ear like this is not a common practice, and here we are with a second occurrence in so short of time. Obviously, it's possible that these murders were committed by two different men, but because of the similarities that we're seeing, I'd say we're dealing with one killer."

"So, we're dealing with a mass murderer," said Kramer.

"Well, if I'm right about this one, I'd say it's Dale Marlowe and this is number five."

"The thing that I don't understand is where is he going?" Kramer asked. "He killed four in Ohio and now this one here in South Carolina. Where in the hell is this guy going?"

"I think he's headed for Florida," said Erv. "If you remember his own wife said that he hated old people and probably thinks they should die. I think he's headed for the state that is famous for old people."

"So, what do you think? Should we head for Florida?"

"Hell, I don't know," said Erv. "Here we are in South Carolina staring at a body. How do we know he won't take a break somewhere else along the way? I think we're chasing a maniac here."

From the other room came the sound of a door opening and closing. "Mr. Meyers, can you come here?" shouted the voice of the officer in charge.

Erv glanced at his brother, and the two of them walked out of the room. The officer was holding the arm of a distressed looking woman. She stepped forward and shook the hands of both Erv and Kramer.

"My name is Aggie Rose," she said with tears glistening in her eyes. "Lucy is...or was my best friend. In fact, we grew up together."

"Obviously, you must have heard what happened to her," said Erv.

"Goodness gracious, it's all over town," she said then pointed a finger. "Is she in there?"

"Yes, I'm afraid so," said Erv. "What can we do for you?"

"Actually, it's what I can do for you," said Aggie. "I think I saw the man who killed her."

Erv glanced at Kramer then turned back to the woman standing in front of him. "Would you like to sit down?"

"Only for a minute," she said taking a seat at the dinner table. "I've got so much to do today what with her dying and such. She had nobody, you know. Just an ex-husband. I'm sure I'll be the one to take care of the business at hand. Ain't too thrilled about doing it. I can tell you that for sure. It would be nice if her ex would take charge, but I know better than that. He is a jerk in capital letters."

"Sounds as if you and Lucy were very close," said Erv.

"We were best of friends more like sisters if you know what I mean. Yes, we were good friends, but we were two totally opposite personalities. You see I'm married to a preacher, and I conduct my life accordingly. You know...I have scruples and lead a morally clean life. Lucy was quite the opposite. Frankly, I could not believe it when she told me that she was getting married. I knew the marriage wouldn't last."

"Are you telling me that she was a bit loose?" Erv asked.

"A bit loose, did you say?" she asked with a smile. "She was a slut to be quite honest about it. Ever since she was a teenager, she would have sex with just about any guy who was interested. Hell, they didn't even have to show interest if she was in the mood. She knew how to entice them. Of course, young teenage boys don't need a lot of encouragement if you know what I mean. Besides all that, I'm going to miss her. She was like a sister to me."

"You said that you saw the man who killed her," said Erv. "Can you tell me where it was that you saw them?"

"Well, my husband and I decided we needed a drink, so we went to a bar that's only a stones throw from our house. We do that from time-to-time. We like to call it a date. Nothing ever happens when we get home, but we have fun while we're there. Anyways, when we walked through the door, I immediately saw her sitting with a strange man. Of course, I pretty much knew what she was up to, so I didn't bother her. Kinda wish I had of now."

"Did you get a good look at the man?" Erv asked.

"Oh, I sure did," she said. "He was downright freaky. I never saw anyone who looked like him. He had the eyes of the devil, I'm telling you. He actually looked like a mass murderer."

Erv reached into his shirt pocket and pulled out a picture of Dale and handed it to her. "Is this the man?"

"Oh, my God!" she shouted. "Yes, this is the man alright. How could you forget a face like that?"

"I want to thank you for all of your help," said Erv as he took the picture from her.

"So, is this the man who killed her?"

"We're not sure," said Erv. "But he is our prime suspect."

"Well, I hope you catch him," said Aggie getting to her feet.

"That is the plan," said Erv as she walked away.

Kramer walked over and stood beside his brother as they both watched Aggie walk away. "What the hell are we dealing with?" Kramer asked.

Erv took a quick glance at Kramer then turned back to the woman as she walked away. "I don't know. She seemed like a decent gal to me," he said with a smile.

"I'm not talking about her. I'm talking about Marlowe," said Kramer. "I've never known anybody like him. It's hard to imagine why he is doing this. I can see when two guys get into an argument, and it leads to a fight. One thing leads to another, and the next thing you know someone gets killed. But this just makes no sense at all. It looks as if he is killing people for the fun of it."

"I've known other guys just like him," said Erv. "They just didn't get a chance to kill as many as this guy has."

"What makes them do it?" Kramer asked. "I can see someone killing another person by getting mad at them or having some kind of skirmish with them but to just kill someone for no good reason is beyond me."

"I don't know much about it either," said Erv with a troubled look on his face. "All I do know is that most of them had a rotten childhood. I don't know if one thing has anything to do with the other, but that's the pattern I've seen."

"No parents?"

"Usually just a mother and she is working a job or two."

"So, the kid grows up not knowing right from wrong," said Kramer.

"Pretty much."

"Kinda scary, isn't it?"

"How so?" Erv asked.

"Well, it seems to be getting worse," said Kramer. "Broken families seem to be getting more and more prevalent. I see it all the time. Back in the old days, two people got married and that was it. They didn't even think about getting a divorce. Oh, they had problems, but they worked them out. Getting a divorce wasn't even an option."

"I got my own theory on that divorce thing," said Erv. "Back in the old days, the man of the house went to work while the wife stayed at home and raised the kids. Today you got men working with women. What do you think is going to happen?"

They both paused.

"So, what do we do now?" Kramer asked.

Erv slowly turned to his brother. "Let's go get this son-of-a-bitch before he kills again."

Nine

It was late morning when Dale Marlowe rolled over and dropped his feet on the floor. He held his aching head with both hands trying to massage away the pain of last night's consumption of liquor. He tried to remember where he was and soon remembered that he had crossed over into Georgia the night before and had stopped at a small motel. He rubbed his head even harder as he tried to remember the events of the last evening. Suddenly, he jumped to his feet. He grabbed his wallet to see how much money was left. He could not remember how much the motel manager had charged him and if the man had taken advantage of his drunken condition. He slowly counted the remaining bills in his wallet and soon realized that only ten dollars were missing. Without doubt that was the amount he must have paid for the room. Funny. It was a nicer room than a ten dollar one. Must have worked out a deal. He couldn't remember, but that's what must have happened.

Dale pulled on his pants and a shirt. He slowly got to his feet and grabbed his head as he stumbled into the kitchen. He searched frantically through the cupboards for something to eat but could find nothing. The place, in general, was filthy, but they managed to keep the cupboards clean.

Dale grabbed his hat and coat and walked out the door. It was time that he got something to eat even if he had to dig something out of a trashcan. It was a small town, and it was no time at all before Dale was downtown. He drove slowly in search of a small diner or restaurant. He was near the other end of town when he came upon a small grocery store. Since he was having a problem finding a place to eat, he decided to buy a few groceries and fix his own meal.

As he opened his car door, he noticed that he had parked in front of a small run-down bar. He paused for only a brief moment to decide whether to buy groceries or have a beer or two. Without further hesitation, he was soon sitting at a table near a window with a bar maid carrying a frosted glass of beer to his table.

As he sat there sipping his beer, it suddenly came to him. Here he was sitting in a small bar sipping on a beer just like many other grown adults, but unlike other grown adults, he had just killed five people in just a few days. Suddenly, the magnitude of what he had done seemed to overtake him. Why was he killing all of these people? Why is he so persistent about the continuation of more killings, and what started all of this?

Not only did his parents neglect him and virtually had nothing to do with him, he never had a friend in school. He was considered an outcast in every grade and was feared by all who knew him. Even when he went to lunch in the school cafeteria, nobody sat at the same table with him. With his tray of food in hand he would slowly approach a table, and as he did the children who were sitting there would get up and find another table to finish their meal. Teachers avoided him and even though he did poorly in school, they would pass him on to the next grade just to eliminate him from their class.

Dale gulped down his beer and opened another one. He began to remember all of the violent and illegal things he had done in his life and began to think that the fault did not rest on his shoulders. If anyone was to blame it was his dysfunctional parents. Not only was he never taught right from wrong, he was born from the genes of two absolute losers in life.

"I can't be blamed for anything I might do that is unlawful," he muttered aloud. "Don't even try it. D'ya hear? Go see my parents. See what losers they are. What did you expect from me? Did ya expect me to turn out good? Expect me to become a priest or something like that? Well, that ain't gonna happen. I'll tell you what I am going to do. I'm going to kill as many innocent victims as I can before they catch me. Ya, that's right. I may not be remembered as a great doctor or some such shit like that, but I'll bet my name will go down in history as the greatest killer of all time."

Dale paused. He suddenly realized that his voice was much louder than he wanted. He scanned the room to find nearly everyone staring at him. He sipped his beer and settled back down in his chair. The others in the room returned to their private conversations.

Dale turned and stared out the window. In spite of the cold weather, it was remarkably a nice day. The sun was shining, and the snow was melting everywhere he looked. Cars were travelling back and forth in front of him, and there were many pedestrians walking in and out of stores.

Then something caught his attention. An older car pulled in front of a small grocery store directly across from the bar. He watched as what seemingly was a beautiful young woman and her young daughter got out of the car. Dale sat up in his chair and leaned forward. From what he could see, she was a young woman about his age. She was tall and slender and was wearing a beautiful pleated skirt. The daughter was wearing a dress as well. She was tall for her young age and exceedingly beautiful.

Dale scrambled to his feet and was out the door. He wasn't quite sure what he was going to do and what her reaction would be to him. He slowed his pace as he entered the grocery store. He looked both ways but could not see her. His hands were shaking as blood pounded through his veins.

Dale grabbed a shopping cart and started down the aisles. As he passed each one, he glanced at the people hoping to find the woman and her child. He was nearly halfway through the store when, suddenly, there she was. She was holding a loaf of bread as she read the label. Dale pushed his cart down the aisle until he was next to her. He picked up a loaf of bread and acted as if he was reading the label as well.

Her name was Laura and her eleven year old daughter's name was Beth. Laura had just ended her only marriage in divorce court and was not really interested in meeting anybody. The marriage had lasted over twelve years but was anything but a perfect marriage. She had become pregnant, and her boyfriend felt a certain responsibility. They were married, and that was virtually the end of a great relationship.

From that point on he was not only mean to her but abusive as well.

Dale smiled at the little girl as she played with an unopened bag of candy. She glanced up at him and forced a return smile. Laura noticed the interaction between the two and smiled at Dale.

"She's a bit bashful," said Laura.

"Well, we have a lot in common, because I am too," said Dale.

"Are you new to the area?" she asked.

"Why do you ask?"

"Oh...well I just don't remember seeing you around town."

"Yeah," he said with conviction. "I'm new around here. Been looking for a job."

"Sorry to hear that," she said. "Jobs around here are a bit hard to find."

"Have you found a place to live?" she asked the smile disappearing from her face.

"No...not really," he muttered. "I'm still looking. Got any suggestions? Maybe you have something available near where you live."

Laura paused. She peered into the eyes of this man standing in front of her. Something was not right. She could not put a finger on it, but there was something about this man that was dangerous if not evil.

"Come on, Beth," she said grabbing her daughter by the arm. "We have to get going."

"Is there something I said?" Dale asked as she nearly ran out the door.

He stopped and watched as she got into her car and sped off. He nearly ran to his car, started it, and slowly followed behind. She turned many corners almost as if she was trying to elude a follower. Dale did his best to remain as far behind her as he could and still not lose track of where she was going.

After several more elusive turns, Laura finally turned into the driveway of a small house at the edge of town. Dale stopped and watched her get out of her car and lead her daughter to the front door. She opened the door and held it open while her daughter entered, then she followed her inside.

Dale got out of his car and ran to the front door. He was not sure if she locked the door or not. He turned the door handle and smiled as the door opened. As he quietly stepped inside, he pulled out his gun. Beth was standing just inside the door.

"Is your father home?" he asked as he scanned the room.

"No," she said with a quiet voice. "It's just mother and me."

As Dale slowly walked closer to Beth, Laura entered the room.

"What are you doing here?" she asked.

Dale pointed his gun at Beth's head. "You do everything I tell you, and nobody gets hurt. Understand?"

Laura stared at the gun pointed at her daughter's head. "I'll do whatever you say," she said with a voice of panic. "Please don't hurt my baby."

"Both of you get into the bedroom," he said with a stern voice.

Laura held Beth close to her side as they slowly walked into the bedroom. They stopped and turned to Dale.

"Got any money?" he asked.

Laura pulled a wallet from her pocket and pulled out a twenty dollar bill. Dale stuffed it in his pocket.

"Take your clothes off," he ordered.

Beth glanced up at her mother.

"Both of you!" he shouted. "Now!"

Laura slowly began to unbutton her blouse. Beth cried as she did the same.

"Please don't hurt my little girl," said Laura wiping the tears from her eyes. "I'll do anything you want me to if you just leave her alone."

"You do what I tell you to do, and neither one of you will get hurt."

They both continued to undress until they were down to their panties. They were both sobbing hysterically while they stood there waiting for their next instructions.

"Don't stop there! Take 'em off!"

They both slid their underpants to the floor and stepped out of them.

"Mommy, I'm scared," said Beth as she covered her crouch with her hands.

"Please don't hurt her," said Laura. "I'm begging you."

"Both of you get down on the floor," Dale demanded.

They both cried hysterically as they stared at each other.

"Get down on that floor and spread your legs!"

"Please don't do this," said Laura. "She is only eleven years old."

"I don't care how old she is just get your asses on the floor," said Dale with an angry voice. "And spread those legs."

They both eased themselves down on the floor and slightly spread their legs. Dale placed his gun on a small table, then took a pair of nylons and tied Laura's hands together. He then smiled as he unzipped his pants and lowered himself on top on Beth. As he slipped one of his hands under her rear end to lift her slightly off the floor, Laura untangled her hands from the nylons and grabbed the gun. She swung the gun with all her might and hit Dale in the head. Blood gushed out and splattered all over the floor.

Dale grabbed his head and slowly managed to get to his feet. As he staggered to the bedroom door, Laura fired two shots that missed him entirely. He ran into the living room and struggled with the door handle. Laura ran after him. She stopped right behind him and pointed the gun at his head. Dale whipped around and grabbed the gun before she was able to pull the trigger. At the same time and without notice, Beth threw a glass ashtray that hit Dale in the head. He staggered backwards several steps, then grabbed the door handle and rushed out of the room.

ᚸ ᚸ ᚸ

It was late in the afternoon when they crossed the state line and entered the state of Georgia. Erv had been driving for several hours and was getting tired. He glanced over at his brother who had been asleep for hours. Erv smiled as he slammed on the brakes. Kramer fell forward and nearly hit his head.

"What happened?" shouted Kramer.

"A deer crossed the road right in front of us," said Erv holding back a smile.

Kramer settled back. "What time is it?"

"It's time we found the Sunset Inn because it's been a long day," said Erv.

"Why are we looking for the Sunset Inn?"

"Oh, I didn't tell you, did I? They are sending us a cell phone, and we can pick it up at the Sunset Inn."

"What the hell is a cell phone?" Kramer asked.

"You don't know what a cell phone is?" asked Erv.

"How the hell would I know?" said Kramer. "I live in a small town in Ohio."

"Cops have had them for years, and they are now coming out for the public. It's a phone that you can carry in your pocket, and you don't need to have it plugged in. You can talk to anyone in the world from just about any where."

"Are you kidding me?" Kramer asked.

"They say that somewhere in the near future everyone will carry a phone with them and will be able to talk to anyone even while they are walking down the street."

Kramer stared at Erv in disbelief. "That's bull shit! It will never happen."

"Why do you say that?"

"Who the hell would want to yak on the phone when you're out in the public?"

"Oh, I'm sure it would be nothing but serious stuff," said Erv. "People wouldn't waste time on it. Take us for example. We will be brought up-to-date on matters concerning Marlowe."

Kramer paused. "I still don't think the general public will have a thing to do with these...what did you call them?

"Cell phones."

"People today have too much going on in their lives to fool around with a cell phone," said Kramer settling back in his seat.

"Thank God," said Erv. "There's the Sunset Inn."

Erv stopped in front of the office. They stepped out of the car, stretched for a moment and then walked inside. An older man was standing behind the counter. He watched as they approached him.

"Is one of you Erv?"

"That would be me."

The old man reached behind the counter and pulled out a small box. "Some cop was in here and said you'd be in here to pick this up."

"Well, thank you," said Erv opening the box.

"That's one of them cell phone things," said the old man.

"You looked inside this box?" asked Kramer.

"Hell, yea. I don't trust nobody these days."

"Kinda big, isn't it?" asked Kramer.

"They say that someday these things will be so small that they will fit right in your shirt pocket," said Erv as he studied the telephone.

"You guys staying here for the night?" asked the old man.

"We're figuring on it," said Kramer.

"I'd think that's the least you could do to repay me for all of this."

"I'm going to step outside and make a phone call," said Erv. "Why don't you get us with a room for the night?"

"Well, you heard the man," said Kramer digging for his wallet.

The old man turned a large book to face Kramer. "Here, sign this for me."

Kramer bent over the book with a pen. "I can't wait to take a shower and get some sleep."

"You boys been on the road for a while?"

"Longer than I'm used to," said Kramer.

"Chasin' somebody?"

"As a matter of fact, we are," said Kramer leaning back. "We're after some guy who has killed several people."

"Oh, my! Hope he ain't from around here."

"He was living in Ohio, and that's where he got started with his killing rampage. We've been chasing him ever since."

"Well, sir, that will be eight dollars for the night."

Kramer pulled out his wallet and opened it. Just as he was about to pull out a ten dollar bill, Erv came back into the room.

"Come on, Kramer," said Erv. "Our day ain't over."

Kramer folded up his wallet and walked to the door. "What happened?"

"Marlowe has been at again."

"Where?"

"Not too far from here," said Erv. "We're finally catching up with him."

"How many did he kill this time?"

"We got a break this time. Seems that he was raping an eleven-year-old girl in front of her mother, and somehow she got her hands free and bashed the guy with something. He ran out and left them behind."

The trip lasted just a little longer than an hour, but the two men were exhausted by the time they reached their destination. Kramer tried to convince Erv that they should find a motel and get some sleep, but Erv wanted to interview the woman while it was fresh in her mind. Kramer tried to convince him that it will probably be years before she will ever forget what happened, but Erv would not give in.

The house was an easy find, and in no time they were sitting in the living room with Laura and her daughter. In spite of the events that had occurred, they both were of reasonable composure.

"I've been told that you have already confirmed that the man who did this was Dale Marlowe," said Erv.

"Oh, it was him alright," said Laura. "They showed me a picture of him, and there was no doubt that was him."

Kramer glanced at Beth and saw that she had a tear streaking down her face. He nudged his brother and pointed at the young girl.

"Is there any chance we could have this conversation with just you?" Erv asked.

Laura turned to her daughter and after seeing the hurt in her eyes asked her to go to her room.

After Beth went to her room and had closed the door, Erv continued. "Can you tell us what he was like? Was he mean and nasty? Did he abuse you in any way?"

"Have you ever seen this man?" asked Laura.

"Just pictures of him," said Erv.

"He is the most alarming and dangerous looking man I have ever seen," she said. "His eyes...there's no way to describe them. They are like the eyes of the devil."

"Was he as mean as he looked?"

"Actually, no, he wasn't," she said. "Or, at least, I should say that he didn't act mean. He was pretty much let's get at it. He didn't come here to talk to us nor did he come here with the intention of beating us. He wanted sex, and that was pretty obvious."

Erv leaned forward. "I don't want to keep you any longer. You've been through enough. I just want to know if there is anything else you can tell me. Did he mention anything about where he was going? Did he mention any names? If you can remember anything at all, it might be helpful."

Laura paused as she stared blankly at the floor. "No...not really. He didn't have much to say. I...I have never in my life wanted to kill someone until this happened. When I hit that man with his own gun, I gave it everything I had. My only regret is that I missed him when I shot at him. I will have to live with that for the rest of my life. I had a chance to kill that son-of-a-bitch and failed."

"Well, if it's any consolation to you, my brother and I are committed to finding this man," said Erv. "You see, this man killed our sister, and there is no way that he is going to get away with that. It would seem that he is on a rampage. If we are right about this, this is the Dale man who has killed many others as well."

"Oh, my God," uttered Laura with a look of amazement. "So, there's a good chance that he would have killed us as well?"

Erv got to his feet. "There's no way of knowing that for sure, but it is obvious that you did the right thing by fighting back."

"Yeah...I guess so."

Erv opened the door, and Kramer followed him out. "Thank you so much, and I hope everything works out for you and your daughter."

"Thank you, and I pray to God that you catch him," she said holding the door open.

"We will give it our best," said Erv and walked away.

"Okay, can we get some sleep?" Kramer asked.

"My God, you are such a weenie," said Erv and left with Kramer behind him.

Ten

Murray Feldman had been a family doctor for over fifty years. At the age of seventy-nine he had finally announced his retirement. In spite of that announcement, he still had visitors knocking on his door complaining of aches and pains and expecting him to cure them. Murray would go through the procedure of telling them that he was retired and could not help them and then would inevitably have them come inside and explain their problems.

It was a cold night in January. It was a habit of Murray to go to bed after the eleven o'clock news, but this night was different. He was caught up in a movie from the thirties. He had seen it many years ago, and, since his memory was not like it used to be, decided to watch it again.

There was a knock on the door. Assuming it was a neighbor or a townsperson with a medical problem, he opened the door. Standing before him was Dale Marlowe who was pointing a gun at him.

"Whoa, what's this all about? Murray asked.

"You gotta sign out in your yard that says you're a doctor," said Dale. "Is that right?"

"Well, I used to be, but I am retired now," said Murray.

He moved to the side as Dale forced his way into the house.

"Sit down," said Dale as he pointed at a chair with his gun.

"What's this all about?" asked Murray as he took a seat.

Dale pulled a kitchen chair over next to Murray. "It's cold out there, and I need a place to warm up."

"Don't you have a home of your own?"

"I did at one time, but those days are over."

Murray frowned at the gun pointing at him. "You can put that thing away. I won't be a problem for you. I'm much too old for that."

"Sorry, but I'm not the kind of man who takes chances," said Dale.

Murray turned and pointed a finger at Dale. "Hey, are you the guy who has been on the loose killing people?"

"Yeah...I guess you could say that," said Dale. "I've knocked out a few."

"You are pretty well known. You made the national news just last night."

"What did they say?"

"Oh, they talked about how many people you've killed," said Murray. "They said something about your killing a woman and one of her brothers is a retired cop. I guess that he and his brother are after you."

"Obviously, they aren't all that good at it."

There was a long pause. Murray began to tap his fingers on the arm of the chair. Suddenly, he turned and pointed a finger at Dale. "You owe me an answer to a question."

"And why is that?" Murray asked.

"Come on...you know why."

"No, I don't. Why do I owe you anything?"

"Well...it's obvious that I'm about to become another addition to your list of victims," said Murray.

"You don't know that," said Dale. "I might let you go."

Murray forced a smile. "We both know that will never happen."

"You don't seem that all that worried about it. Most people would be begging me not to hurt them."

"Oh, I don't know," said Murray with a warm smile. "I've had a good life. I was a doctor for most of my life. Can't even remember how many people I've helped, the babies I've brought into this world. It's been a good life, and I'm proud of what I have done."

"Ah, you doctors are all alike," said Dale. "You charge high fees and become rich."

Murray laughed aloud. "You cannot be serious. "This is a small town. There is very little money here. Half of my patients at best would bring me a sack of corn or beans that they picked from their farm fields. They had no money. They did the best they could."

"So, what you're telling me is you ain't got no money?"

Murray scanned the room. "Hell, this house isn't even half paid for." He then muttered, "Guess I won't have to worry about that anymore."

Dale leaned back in his chair and placed his gun in his lap. "Got any idea why you decided to become a doctor?"

"Oh, I don't know. I was born with the interest and desire to be a doctor. I guess it was God who made me this way."

"So, you believe in God?" Dale asked with a sarcastic grin.

"Why? You don't?"

"Are you kidding me? You're trying to tell me that this God guy created all of the planets and human beings?"

"Well, how do you think this all got started? How did all the planets come about?"

Ah, Hell," said Dale. "I have no idea."

"That is the point," said Murray. "Outside of the Ten Commandments, all God ever asks of us is to simply believe in Him. He's not asking for miracles from us. All He is asking is to believe in Him."

"It's all a bunch of shit," said Dale leaning back in his chair. "I didn't believe in superman, and I damn sure don't believe in God."

"That's because your brain as well as everyone else's is only made to get you around here on earth. You know to zip up your pants after taking a leak. You know not to belch at the table. Well, maybe that's a bit much for you. The point is we are very limited in our thinking process. Albert Einstein once said that you have to be a fool not to believe that thought went into all this. You know I am a doctor, and I am amazed at the human body. Do you realize that your elbows have a sac that secretes a lubrication to keep your elbows from hurting? It is so fine and slippery that we humans cannot duplicate it. There are body parts inside you that man doesn't even understand how they work. For example, your heart started beating while you were still inside your mother. It will keep on beating for another eighty years and then suddenly stop. Have you ever wondered how that thing keeps beating? Of course not. Our minds are limited. We think we know everything, but we don't have a clue."

There was a pause. Dale stared blankly at Murray as if deep in thought.

"That's interesting, Doc...I'll have to admit. Never thought I'd see the day when someone would make me stop and think."

Murray turned and pointed a finger at Dale.

"Tell me something," said Murray. Do you have any idea why you kill people?"

"No...not really."

"Are you jealous that other people have money, and you don't?

"No."

"Most people have families. Do you?"

"I used to."

"Let's talk about your mother and father," said Murray. "What can you tell me about them?"

Dale leaned back once again. "No, we aren't going there."

"Oh, so I hit a nerve," said Murray. "Let me guess...your mother was mean to you, and your father left home."

Dale said nothing. His face went blank as he stared at the ceiling.

"Don't feel bad," said Murray. "This kind of thing happens to many people, but because you had a bad childhood doesn't give you the right to kill others."

Dale turned to Murray and stared at him with a look of anger. Suddenly, he lifted his gun and pointed into Murray's ear. The explosion from the gun was loud. The bullet tore though his ear and blew part of the other side of his head onto the floor. Blood squirted from the cavity far enough that it hit the wall. Murray shook uncontrollably for a few seconds and then came to rest. His head slowly bowed down as if he were asleep in his chair.

Dale took a last look at the dead man, got up and left the house.

⋏ ⋏ ⋏

"I wish this guy would sleep at night like normal people," said Kramer as he turned down a side street.

"I just wish this guy would stop killing people," said Erv.

"By the way, who was it this time?"

"Some guy named Murray something or other," said Erv. He was a retired doctor, and believe it or not, he was shot in the ear and he is sitting upright in his chair."

"Well, at least we don't have to wonder who did it," said Kramer. "Who found him?"

"Apparently, the next door neighbor heard the shot and called the police," said Erv.

"I don't mind telling you that this is becoming a real nightmare," said Kramer as he scanned street signs.

"What do you mean?"

"The killings," said Kramer. "It just seems to go on forever. It truly is a nightmare going from one to another. I thought I had seen everything until this happened."

"Well, I can't blame you," said Erv. "I was a cop for most of my life, and I thought I had seen it all until this began. It just makes you wonder about this guy. What happened in his life that made him turn to this kind of violence? Was he born this way or did something happen to him when he was growing up? I hope some day I get the opportunity to ask him that question."

"I never thought I would see the day when I would say this, but all I want to see is his dead body," said Kramer. "That guy needs to die. I don't know what his problem is, and I don't care. He needs to go."

"I won't argue with you on that comment," said Erv.

"Here's the street of the doctor's house," said Kramer as he turned down the street.

Nearly a block down the street was police cars with flashing lights parked in front of a house.

"Guess we don't have to check house numbers," said Erv.

Kramer stopped the car in front of the house, and they both got out. A policeman approached them as they walked towards the house.

"Is one of you Erv Meyers?" asked the policeman.

"That would be me," said Erv.

"Go on inside. They are waiting for you."

As they walked inside, a policeman approached them and told them that they needed to know when they were finished with the investigation so that they could remove the body. Erv and Kramer walked slowly into the next room and found an older man sitting in a leather chair. His head was bent over as if he was asleep.

"Do you suppose that's him?" Kramer asked.

"That is the victim," said a policeman standing by the door. "He was a doctor, and his name is Murray Feldman."

"He looks as if he is asleep," said Kramer.

"From this angle, you are right," said the policeman. "You need to see the other side of his head...or what's left of it."

Kramer glanced at Erv.

"Well, here we go again," said Erv as he started across the room.

They both walked slowly across the room until they were standing directly in front of Murray. They paused for a moment then eased over to the other side. Part of Murray's brains was hanging loosely from the hole in the side of his head. Dried blood was caked down his side. There was blood splattered on the wall, and a pool of blood on the floor. Erv studied both sides of his head and then stepped back.

"Well, he's at it again," said Erv. "The ear must be the bull's eye for this guy. Did you happen to find any evidence at all?"

"Not a thing. Do you think that Marlowe guy did it?" asked the policeman.

"I'm sure of it," said Erv. "I swear he does this to leave his mark. That way we all know that he was the killer."

"I hear you guys have been following him," said the policeman. "How many does this one make?"

"To tell you the truth, I'm not sure," said Erv. "We think he has killed six of them, but who knows how many have not been discovered."

"How did you get stuck with the job of finding him?"

"We volunteered right after he killed our sister," said Erv.

The policeman paused then muttered, "Sorry...I will leave you gentlemen alone for now." He then walked out of the room.

Erv bent over and scoured the room looking for evidence.

"We gotta get this guy," said Kramer.

"Hey, we're doing everything we can," said Erv. "There's no way of knowing where he's going or who's next on the list.

The only thing I can tell you for sure is that we are going to catch him. That's for sure."

"Well, I hope you're right," said Kramer.

"Let's get out of here," said Erv as he walked towards the doorway.

Eleven

It was January 27, 1982. Sherry Jones had dealt with a severe cold for over two weeks and was finally over it. Her dying grandmother was in the hospital, and Sherry felt bad that she could not spend any time with her for fear of transferring the cold to her. Today was different though. Today she felt as if the cold had subsided enough that she could go to the hospital and see her grandmother.

Sherry was a 37-year-old native of Pascagoula, Mississippi. She had a passion for staying at home and rarely left her house for any reason. If she did leave the house and would be gone when her husband, John came home from work at four o'clock in the afternoon, she always left a note to explain to him where she was and when she should be coming home.

It was nearly noon when she drove across town to visit her grandmother at the hospital. As she checked in at the desk, she was told that her grandmother was unconscious, yet still alive. Sherry entered her room and was sickened at the site of how much her grandmother had degraded. She sat down next to her and spoke softly to her with the hope of her responding by opening her eyes and smiling at her.

It was two o'clock in the afternoon. Sherry had tried her best to get her grandmother to respond but to no avail. Besides, it was time to go home and prepare a meal for her husband. She stopped at the desk to ask a few questions and was soon on her way home.

ㅅ ㅅ ㅅ

The next day and just a few blocks down the road, Deputy Sheriff David Saunders returned to work after taking a week's vacation. There were several other deputy sheriffs in the office when he arrived.

"Well, look who's back," said Officer John Stiles.

"Good morning, guys," said Saunders. "I can't say that I'm all that thrilled to be back."

"Did you go any place last week?" Stiles asked.

"Nope. In fact I didn't even leave the house," said Saunders. "I painted one of the bedrooms. That took two days, and the rest of the time I watched television and played with the wife."

"All together that sounds kinda boring," said Stiles.

"What? Messing around with my wife? I'll tell her you said that, and the next time you come over to play poker, be careful when she brings you a drink."

Saunders walked over to a desk and picked up a sheet of paper. "I see we have a missing person report."

"Yeah, some woman was reported missing, and it's only been one day," said Stiles. "I'll bet anything she's already back home."

The smile on Saunders' face disappeared. His hands started to shake as he studied the missing person report.

"Are you okay?" Stiles asked.

"Do you know anything more about this missing woman?" asked Saunders.

"Not really. It just came through a few minutes ago. Why?"

"I don't know. I can't explain it."

"Explain what?"

"I got this feeling that I should go and find her."

Stiles forced a smile. "Are you kidding?"

"I know it sounds crazy, but I have this feeling that I was meant to find this woman," said Saunders with a stern voice.

The smile disappeared from Stiles' face. "I don't think I've ever seen you like this. This thing has really grabbed you, hasn't it?"

"I've never had anything like this happen to me," said Saunders. "I have to check this out."

"Well, let's go," said Stiles.

"What do you mean? Are you coming with me?"

"I gotta see how this turns out," said Stiles walking towards the door. "Besides, there ain't nothing else going on."

They both walked outside and got in one of the sheriff cars with Saunders driving. For some unknown reason, he drove a short distance out of town on Highway 90. He turned down a side road, drove for another mile then turned onto a dirt road. A short distance later they came upon a small cemetery. Saunders slowly turned into it and parked the car.

"What the hell are you doing?" asked Stiles.

Saunders slowly turned to Stiles. "She's here."

"What?"

"She is somewhere in this cemetery," said Saunders.

Stiles turned and looked out the window of the car. "I didn't even know this cemetery was here."

"Neither did I," said Saunders.

Stiles opened the car door. "Man, you are acting really weird."

It was a small cemetery filled with a scattering of old and decrepit tombstones. There, lying among a pile of empty beer bottles was the dead body of Sherry Jones. She was naked from the waist down and her blouse was torn open.

"Oh, my God," muttered Saunders.

"I'd say she's been raped," said Stiles.

Saunders bent down and examined her left ear. He then leaned over to find a pool of blood and part of her skull missing.

"Makes you wonder, doesn't it?" Saunders asked.

"What's that?"

"Did he rape her before or after he shot her?"

"You know after all of these years you would think that I could get used to seeing such a thing," said Stiles. "This ain't the first murdered person I've seen, and yet it gets to me every time."

"Hey, if this kind of thing didn't bother you, I wouldn't have anything to do with you," said Saunders.

"Wait a minute!" said Stiles. "This woman was shot in the head. There is a guy who has been killing people by shooting them in the ear. I guess he travels from state-to-state leaving dead bodies behind him. There is a team of guys trying to catch him, and we're supposed to call them when we find a body of someone who was shot in the ear."

"Not a problem," said Saunders. "Let's get at it."

⁂

It was a small town in the upper part of the state of Florida. Two men took a seat at a table in a small diner. An older woman with a harsh and deep voice and a cigarette hanging from her mouth set two plates of breakfast food on the table.

"Anything else I can get ya?" she said.

Erv held out his hands. "Maybe, something to drink? Water would be fine."

"Yeah, yeah," she muttered and walked away.

"I wonder if that means we're going to get something to drink," said Kramer.

"I'm not going to push the issue," said Erv. "She scares the hell out of me."

"I don't think she expects a tip from us," said Kramer.

"Good thing."

Kramer stuck a fork in his fried potatoes then turned to Erv. "In all of your years as a cop, did you ever encounter something like this?"

"What d'ya mean?"

"A guy on a killing rampage like this," said Kramer. "I guess that's a dumb question seeing as how we live in such a small town."

"We've had a couple bad guys over the years but nothing like this."

"Well, tell me something, Brother," said Kramer leaning back in his chair. "Why in the world did you become a cop, for God's sakes? We don't have cops in the family. What provoked you to do such a thing?"

Erv smiled. "You make it sound like I did something bad."

"How many times have you bitched about the fact that your life is on the line, and they don't pay you shit? Why didn't you find something else to do?"

"Do you remember when Jessie Wells overturned her car into a ditch, and the car caught on fire? I got her out of that car just seconds before it exploded," said Erv still smiling. "Remember when Mark Smith was out running in the forest and got lost? I was the one who found him."

"Yeah, I heard he bought a treadmill shortly after that," said Kramer.

"It's not that I expect to change the world or make an influence in people's lives," said Erv. "I just wanted to help somebody along the way. That's all."

"Oh, so, handing out traffic tickets is helping mankind," said Kramer.

"I've caught guys doing sixty miles per hour in front of the school right when the kids were leaving," said Erv. "They were lucky I only gave them a ticket. I wanted to beat the shit out of them."

"What about this guy?" Kramer asked. "Do you think we will ever catch him?"

"Oh, we'll catch him alright," said Erv. "He's gotta make a mistake somewhere along the line, and we'll be there."

Kramer leaned back. "Well, I have to say this much. So far, he's done a very good job of eluding us. This guy ain't no genius, but he's no dummy either."

Just as Erv leaned back in his chair, there came a ringing sound that gave a puzzled look to both men.

"What the hell is that?" Kramer asked.

Erv reached under the table and pulled up a small bag.

"It's that telephone thingy," said Erv. "Can you believe that? You don't have to plug it into anything. It's kinda like the phones in our police cars."

"Better answer it before they give up on ya," said Kramer.

Erv stood and walked outside the diner before answering the phone. In less than a minute, he returned to his chair and laid the phone on the table.

"You ain't going to believe this," said Erv with a look of anger. "That son-of-a-bitch has killed another one, this time in Mississippi."

Kramer scooted back his chair. "Are we heading out?"

"No...not this time," said Erv staring blankly at his brother. "I told them to go ahead and do their thing. They found a woman in a graveyard. She had been shot in the ear. There's no doubt in my mind who did it. It's just a waste of time. Besides, I still think he is heading for Florida, and we're going to be here ready to catch the bastard."

"Sounds good to me," said Kramer. "Let's get the hell out of here."

⋏ ⋏ ⋏

It was late in the evening on January 29, 1982. In a small bar in downtown Baton Rouge, Louisiana, Dale Marlowe stepped inside and took a seat at the bar. Nick Lepus was 61 years old and had owned the bar for most of his life. He had just bought a small house outside of town and was planning to finally retire. Nick loved his bar, but he spent so many hours each week working there that he never had time for relaxation or spending time on a vacation. Nick had saved all of his money over the years and had in fact paid cash for his new house. He was happy with his life but needed to retire.

"What can I get ya?" Nick asked the man sitting at the bar.

"Gimme me a beer," said Marlowe. "Make it two beers."

"Tough day?" Nick asked as he slid two beers in front of his customer.

"Yeah, you could say that."

"Well, I will leave you alone," said Nick. "If you need anything, I will be sitting over there with my brother."

Nick's brother, Adam, had spent most of his life helping Nick at his bar. Adam had his own job but had spent his weekends and evenings helping his brother. He never accepted any pay but helped himself to a drink now and then.

"Did you see that guy sitting over there at the bar?" asked Nick.

Adam turned and glanced at Marlowe. "Not really. Why? What's wrong with him?"

"I don't know," said Nick. "But he has the weirdest look on his face, and his eyes...his eyes are like the eyes of the devil. He is one scary looking dude."

Adam finished his beer. "I was heading for home. Want me to stick around?"

Nick waved his hand at his brother. "Oh, no. I can handle the likes of him. Besides, I have a forty-five back behind the bar."

Adam got to his feet. "Getting about time to close up anyhow."

Nick followed his brother across the room. He glanced at his watch. "Yeah, you are right about that. I think I will lock the door behind you."

Adam opened the door and turned to look at Marlowe sitting at the bar. "Are you sure you want me to go?"

Nick pushed his brother out the door. "Go home," he said and locked the door behind him.

"Did I hear you lock the door?" Marlowe asked without turning around.

Nick walked across the room and went behind the bar. He glanced down at his gun. It was laying knee high on a shelf in front of Marlowe. He picked up a damp rag and began wiping the surface of the bar.

"Yeah, it's getting about time to close up," said Nick as he moved slowly towards his gun.

Marlowe pulled out his pistol and pointed it at Nick. "I get the idea you were expecting this."

"No...not really," said Nick raising his hands chest high. He then glanced down at his gun that was by now only inches away.

"Don't even think about it," said Marlowe. "I know all you bar owners have a gun somewhere hidden behind the bar. It's usually about midway which would mean that yours is damn close to both of us. The big mistake you guys make is you usually put a shotgun down there. A shotgun is a great weapon. That's for sure. But it takes twice as long to get it up here to serve any purpose."

Nick said nothing.

"Where the hell is yours?" Marlowe asked as he leaned over the bar. "Well, I'll be darn. You've got a pistol right in the middle of the bar. At least you were smart enough to use a handgun rather than a shotgun."

"What do you want from me?" Nick asked. "Do you want money? I'll give you all that I have in the cash register."

Marlowe waved the gun at the register. "What the fuck do you think I'm doing here? Empty that cash register and hand it over."

Nick opened the drawer and pulled all of the money out. With a shaking hand he handed the money to Marlowe.

"Give me the key to the front door," said Marlowe with his hand held out.

"You're the guy who has been killing people, aren't you?" Nick asked as he handed him the key.

"Yeah. How did you know about me?"

"You're all over the news."

"Oh, yeah? I didn't know I was so popular."

"I wouldn't use the word popular," said Nick with a soft voice.

"Notorious?"

"That would be a better word to use."

"You seem like a nice guy," said Marlowe. "Any plans for the future?"

"Well, yes," said Nick as he slowly dropped his hands onto the bar. "I'm planning on selling this place and retire. Been working all my life. It's time to lean back and enjoy life."

Marlowe smiled. "I don't get it. Here I am pointing a gun at you, and you don't seem a bit scared. Hell, you act like we're old friends."

"Hey, if it's my time to go there's nothing I can do about it," said Nick in a candid manner. "God has a plan for every one of us, and it's all up to Him."

"Oh, so you're one of them Bible totin' kinda guys," said Marlowe.

"I believe in God, if that's what you mean."

"Well, if there is a God, why is He letting me kill people?"

"Oh, I don't understand any of that stuff," said Nick. "I don't even think the human brain was ever meant to understand much more than getting around here on earth."

"If God is in control, why did He make the likes of me?" Marlowe asked. "Here I am killing people right and left. Was that God's plan for me?"

"I have no idea, but I'll bet He has a plan for your afterlife," said Nick with a slight smile.

Marlowe paused then a look of anger swept his face. "You're saying that I'm going to Hell, aren't you?"

Nick said nothing.

"Well, guess what? Maybe I'll see you there," said Marlowe as he jerked the gun towards Nick's head. "But you're going there first."

Nick turned his head and quickly closed his eyes.

Marlowe lightly touched a spot behind Nick's left ear with the barrel of the gun. He pulled the trigger, and a loud report echoed throughout the building. The bullet tore through his head and exited out the other side sending a violent spray of blood across the room. Nick's life ended by the time he hit the floor. Marlowe bent over and fired three more shots into the lifeless body then slowly walked out of the building.

⋏ ⋏ ⋏

It was an early morning in a small town in Florida. The temperature was in the low 50's which seemed rather cold to the local residents but to Erv and Kramer who had spent all of their lives in Ohio it was uncommonly warm.

Erv stepped out of the shower and grabbed a towel. It felt good to finally clean up and enjoy the warmth. There was a part of him that wanted to go back home and turn it all back to the local police. There were over five hundred members of the police force from different states searching for Marlowe. If he hadn't killed a member of his family, Erv would certainly be home watching the news. It all seemed like an endless nightmare. In all of his years of police work, Erv had never had experienced such a rampage of violence. What possessed a man to kill nine people, and they had no reason to believe that he was finished.

Erv had thoughts of giving up and returning to his home in Ohio, but there was a part of him that sensed that he was supposed to be the one to catch this incredibly vicious man. He could not explain it and had no idea why, but he felt compelled to be the one who would end this nightmare.

The door to the bathroom opened slightly, and Kramer stuck his head inside. "He got another one," he said.

"Where was it?"

"He shot a bartender in Baton Rouge, Louisiana."

"How did you find out?" Erv asked.

"I got a call from a cop in that town," said Kramer. "He wants to know if we are coming over there to take a look."

Erv paused. "Tell him that we won't be coming there. They can conduct their own investigation. We already know the results."

"Do you still think he is heading for Florida?"

"Why do you ask?"

"Well, he seems to be jumping from state to state," said Kramer.

"Oh, you're right there, but where do most people go during the winter?" Erv asked. "I think his goal is to get down here, but for whatever reason he needs to kill a few on the way. Maybe this is the way he practices for the big event. You know...like a baseball pitcher warming up for the big game."

"Don't even joke about what he's doing," said Kramer. "He is one sick bastard, and I want to see him dead."

"Well, there's one thing we agree on."

"Get dressed, and let's go get something to eat. I'm starving," said Kramer and closed the door.

Twelve

Vernon Johnson was 27 and an escapee from a jail in a small town in Mississippi. He had served a sentence in prison for robbery and was now wanted for burglary. He had spent most of the week hitchhiking his way towards Florida. He knew that he was most likely being pursued but was confident that he could get lost in the highly populated state of Florida.

Nineteen year old Robert Daily had become friends with Johnson and had decided to follow along with him on his way to Florida. He had nothing in his life to hold him back, and he had always wanted to see what Florida was all about. He had always enjoyed his childhood spent in a small town in Mississippi but decided that it was time to change his life.

As the two young men walked along a country road, they spotted an older car in the ditch. Steam was pouring from under the hood. It was if the car had been involved in an accident, and yet there was no other vehicle in sight. They walked up to the side of the car and looked inside. There was a young woman sitting behind the wheel with a look of frustration.

"Are you okay?" Vernon asked.

"Yeah, I'm alright," she said with a look of exasperation. "It's this friggin' car that has the problem."

"What's wrong with it?" asked Vernon glancing at the hood of the car.

"I don't know. I was driving down this back road when all of a sudden there was this smoke pouring out from under the hood."

"There's a gizmo under the hood that controls the heat of the engine," said Vernon. "It's a cheap little device but goes bad very often. The next thing you know your car is overheating."

"How much is that going to cost me?" she asked.

"They only cost a few bucks, and I can install it for you."

"That's awesome," she said. "Thank you so much."

"What's you name?" Vernon asked.

"Jones," she said. "Frances Jones. What's your name?"

"My name is Vernon Johnson, and this is my buddy, Bob Daily. His name is Bob, but he likes to go with the Robert thing. I think it makes him feel more important."

Frances turned to Robert. "Nice to meet you..."

"Call me Bob. Trust me. I'm okay with that name."

"Are you guys hungry?" she asked.

"We are starving," said Robert.

Frances turned to the backseat and grabbed a paper bag. "I packed a bunch of sandwiches. Help yourselves."

Vernon grabbed two sandwiches and handed one to Robert. "So, tell me, where are you going? You certainly packed enough food to last you for a while."

The smile on her face disappeared.

"I just left my husband. I couldn't take him anymore. I have decided to move to Florida. Everyone else seems to move there."

"Was your husband mean to you?" Vernon asked.

"Not all the time, but when he got drunk he was one person to stay away from."

"Did he beat you?"

"Oh, yeah. More than just a few times. He would hit me just for the fun of it. I've never owned a gun. Hell, I've never even held one in my hands, but if I had one he would be dead today."

"Well, sounds like you're doing the right thing," said Robert.

Frances paused as she turned away. "Not really."

"Why? What's wrong?" Vernon asked.

"I had to leave my baby girl behind," she said with tears falling down her face. "She's only five years old, but I had to leave her at least until I can get settled in a new home."

"Will the old man take care of her?" Vernon asked.

"Yes…I will give him that much credit. He is a very good father. Too bad he sucks as a husband. What about you two? Where are guys going?"

"We're going to try and find a place here in Florida to live," said Vernon. "Tired of the snow and need a change."

"Well, can you fix my car?" Frances asked.

"We're going to need a part," said Vernon. "Maybe there's a town up ahead where we can buy the part."

"And you say that it doesn't cost much?"

"No, they are very inexpensive and easy to install."

"Well, I guess we should get going," she said.

Nearly an hour passed. The three of them had walked nearly five miles when they decided to stop for a rest. The heat of the day had now reached nearly a record temperature. Even though the three of them had lived in the southern state of Mississippi none of them had experienced such heat for that time of year.

They rested for several minutes and were about to resume their walk when a car appeared down the road. It was heading in the same direction driven by a man who would end their lives.

"Need a ride?" Marlowe asked as he stopped his car beside them.

They all looked at each other.

"Sure," said Vernon as they opened the back doors and slid inside.

"Where are you all going?" Marlowe asked.

"No place in particular," said Vernon. "We're looking for a place to buy a part for this girl's car."

"What's the matter with her car?"

"Over heats," said Vernon.

"I saw a car parked along side of the road several miles back there," said Marlowe. "Was that it?"

"Green Ford?"

"Yeah. That was it."

"I think it needs that gizmo that stops an engine from overheating," Said Vernon.

"Yeah...probably so," said Marlowe. "There should be a town up ahead. Maybe we can find a store that sells car parts."

"Sounds great."

"So, did you kids grow up here in Florida?" Marlowe asked.

"No, we're all from Mississippi," said Vernon.

"Can't believe you're leaving Mississippi," said Marlowe. There ain't nothing wrong with that state. Hell, it's even better than Florida."

"We got nothing against our home state," said Vernon. "We just want a change. We might even go back to Mississippi if we don't like Florida."

"Does anybody know what you're doing?" Marlowe asked.

Vernon glanced at the other two. "What do you mean?"

"Does anyone of you have a parent, wife or husband who knows where you're going?"

"Why do you ask?"

"Just curious," said Marlowe.

Vernon turned to the others with a wide-eyed look. "Yeah...we all have someone back home that knows what we're doing."

Marlowe glanced into the rear view mirror and saw Vernon whispering to the others. With the look on Vernon's face, it was obvious that he was suspicious that something was wrong. He turned down a dirt road that led into a small forest.

"Where are we going?" Vernon asked.

Marlowe said nothing. Once he had entered the confines of the forest, he pulled the car over to the side of the road and turned off the engine.

"What the hell is going on?" Vernon asked with an angry voice.

Marlowe turned and pointed his handgun at Vernon. "All three of you get the hell out of the car."

Vernon got out of the car and held the door open for the other two.

Marlowe pointed his gun at Robert and Frances. "You two sit down on the ground over there. He then tossed a roll of duct tape to Vernon and told him to tape their hands and feet. When he had finished, Marlowe taped Vernon's hands and feet as well.

At the onset, Frances had begun to cry. By this time, she was screaming loudly trying to alert anyone that might be nearby. Marlowe became more and more irritated at her. He told her repeatedly to stop screaming but to no avail. He pointed his gun at her which made her scream all the louder.

Marlowe placed the opening of the gun barrel in her ear. Frances could not move since her head was lying on the ground. He pulled the trigger. There was a loud report. The bullet tore a hole in her skull splattering blood on everything around her including Marlowe and the young men lying next to her. Marlowe tried desperately to wipe the blood from his face. He removed his handkerchief and wiped his face repeatedly until the handkerchief was soaked in blood.

Marlowe's desperation turned to anger. He leaned forward and pointed the gun at Robert's head and pulled the trigger. More blood splattered everywhere. He then turned to Vernon who by now was screaming as well. He moved forward until he was next to the young man. Marlowe pointed the gun at Vernon's head and quickly pulled the trigger. The bullet tore through one side of his head and exited out the other side. Marlowe got to his feet. For a few seconds he stared at the three dead bodies then turned and walked away.

入 入 入

It was February 7th, and Kramer had just ordered his breakfast in a small diner when Erv walked over to the table.

"Forget about your breakfast," said Erv. "We got to go."

Kramer stared at his brother with a look of shock. "You can't be serious! I just ordered my breakfast."

"Marlowe just killed three kids, and their bodies are only a couple miles away," said Erv. "We're going to catch that son-of-a-bitch. I can just feel it."

Kramer glanced down at the empty table and then turned to Erv. "Alright... Let's go."

It was a short drive taking them less than a half hour to reach the scene of the crime. There were several police cars already there with their lights flashing. Erv parked behind one of the cars, and they both got out.

"You must be the Meyers brothers," said one of the policemen.

"I'm Erv and this is Kramer."

"Well, we haven't touched a thing," said the policeman. They are all yours. When you are done, we will take care of the bodies."

The two men walked slowly over to the scene of the crime. As they stepped to the other side of a tree, they looked down on three dead bodies and a sea of blood.

"Good Lord!" said Kramer. "Do you believe this?"

"In all my years I have never seen such a sight," said Erv. "I once read that a bullet in the head rather than one in the body shoots out twice as much blood. I don't know why. Must have something to do with the brain."

Erv leaned over each of the dead bodies and studied their wounds. "Well, no question who did it. They were all shot in the side of the head. That seems to be his trademark."

"Well, you were right about him heading for Florida," said Kramer. "Think he will stay here?"

"Oh, I'm sure of it," said Erv. "And I'll tell you something. We are going to get this bastard and real soon."

Kramer paused as he stared at the dead bodies. "I cannot understand how someone could do something like this. These are young kids with their lives ahead of them, and now...now they're headed for the grave."

"Makes you wonder, doesn't it?" Erv asked. "What goes through the brain of a guy who would do something like this? Was he born like this or has life created him to do something like this? Some people simply have a horrible childhood and seem to want to take it out on others."

"I don't know," said Kramer. "But when we catch up with this guy, I hope he pulls his gun on us because I really would love to put one in his ear."

Erv smiled. "Come on. We have work to do."

The two men got into their car and drove down a country road trying to emulate what Marlowe would do and where he might go. There was small talk between the two of them, but morale was high. They both had the feeling that they were closing in on a dangerous man who had killed twelve people. After nearly an hour of driving, they came upon a small town nestled in the midst of a deep forest. Erv parked the car in front of a small and run down motel.

"Why are we stopping here?" Kramer asked.

"I'm guessing that Marlowe stopped here too," Erv said.

"What makes you think that?"

"I don't know...just a hunch," Erv said with a smile. "If I'm right though we're going to finally catch that son-of-a-bitch."

"The one thing that we do know is we are getting closer," said Kramer.

"Let's check into this sleazebag motel and tell him who we are and what we're doing here. I want everyone to know us and the fact that we're after Marlowe," said Erv. "Do you still have those pictures of him?"

Kramer picked up a folder containing pictures of Marlowe, and the two men got out of the car. It was an old and rundown motel. An old man sat a desk with a cigar hanging from his mouth.

"Can I help you guys?" he asked.

"Yeah, we need a room for the night," said Erv searching the desk. "What's your name?"

"Why? What's it to ya?"

"I'm a cop, and I need to know you for a very short time."

"Jim...Jim Towle is my name."

"Jim, my name is Erv and this is Kramer. We've been trying to find the guy who has been killing people across the country."

"Oh, that Marlowe guy," said Jim.

"That's the one."

"Yeah, everybody is talking about that guy," said Jim. "So, why are you down here? I thought that guy was killing people in the northern states."

"We think he has moved down here," said Erv. "In fact, I have a strong feeling he is right here in your town. Are there anymore motels in this town?"

"There's one on the other side of town. It ain't as nice as this one," said Jim.

Erv glanced at Kramer with a smile. "Has anybody else checked in here today?"

"Nope. You're the only one."

"I need you to do me a favor," said Erv. "You probably know most everyone in town. Can you contact people including the owner of that other motel and tell them that we think Marlowe is in town, and if they see anybody who fits the description or is simply a stranger in town tell them to call us?"

"Yeah. I can do that," said Jim. "I ain't the best of friends with the owner of that other motel, but I'll call him."

"Just be careful if you see this guy," said Erv.

"Oh, I ain't scared of nobody," said Jim with a smile. "I got a gun right here under my desk."

"Dale Marlowe has shot twelve people in the head," said Erv. "One more makes no difference to him."

Jim leaned back. His eyes widened. "Oh…well, I will surely let you know if he shows up."

⅄ ⅄ ⅄

It was late in the evening. The sun had already gone down, and with the lack of moonlight, the sky was exceptionally dark. Erv and Kramer had spent the day trying to notify everyone in town of their existence and where they were staying with hopes that if Marlowe was in town or was about to enter the small village, someone might let them know.

For the first time in weeks, the two men felt at rest. For days they had been chasing what seemed to be an extraordinarily elusive man. Just as they would catch up to one of his victims, they would get a call that would direct them to another dead person who had been shot in the head. It seemed like a constant chase just to find the latest body rather than the killer.

It was nearly ten o'clock. Both Erv and Kramer were asleep as they sat in their chairs in front of the television when the telephone rang.

"Hello," said Erv grabbing the phone.

Kramer leaned forward and watched as his brother took in a message. He could tell something positive was being said from the expression on Erv's face.

"Okay and thanks for the call," said Erv then hung up the phone.

"Well?" said Kramer.

Erv jumped to his feet. "We got him. He's staying at that nasty motel on the other side of town. He just checked in."

"Well, let's go," said Kramer.

It was a short drive to that side of town but seemed like forever to the two men. Erv purposely drove slowly so as not to arouse suspicion. The last thing they needed was town residents following them to watch the events as they unfolded. Both men anticipated at the very least a shoot out with this man.

As they approached the motel, Erv slowed the car down until they were slowly passing the different rooms.

"What room is he in?" Kramer asked.

"He's in room 110. There it is," said Erv as he parked the car in front of the room next to it.

"I see a light on," said Kramer.

"Can you see Marlowe in there?" Erv asked.

Kramer leaned forward. "Can't see through that curtain."

Erv pulled out his gun. "Let's go get the son-of-a-bitch."

They both got out of the car and eased the doors closed. Kramer pulled out his gun as well. They slowly walked to the door with the number 110 on it.

"What about a backdoor?" whispered Kramer. "Do you want me to go around to the back?"

"The owner told me that there are no backdoors," said Erv. "What are you going to do? Are you going to knock on the door or bust the door down?"

"We'll knock on the door and shout out that it's a pizza delivery. There ain't a man alive who wouldn't open the door," said Erv.

"Damn I'm nervous," said Kramer. "How 'bout you?"

"Hell yes," said Erv. "You'd have to be a bit crazy not to be. Okay, here we go."

They slowly and cautiously walked over to the door. Kramer's gun began to shake in his hand. They stopped with one on each side of the door.

"Pizza!" shouted Erv.

From the corner of his eye, Erv saw a shadow walk up to the window and the curtain pulled back slightly.

"He just saw us," said Erv.

Suddenly they could hear someone running to the back of the room.

"We should have gotten a key from the owner," said Kramer.

"Too late now," said Erv. "Let's break it down."

Both men slammed the door several times before it finally busted open. They both slowly eased themselves into the room with guns pointed. There was nobody there. They scoured the room looking behind chairs but could not find anyone.

"The bathroom," said Erv. "The door is closed."

They both walked slowly over to the door one on each side of it. Erv slowly turned the handle, and to his surprise it opened. Kramer kicked the door until it was completely open. Erv cautiously peeked around the corner. He could see nearly all of the room except for the area behind the door. Then he saw it. There was a small window that was head high at one end of the room. The window was open.

Erv rushed inside and scoured the room. "The son-of-a-bitch crawled out that window. God knows where he's at now."

"Well he couldn't have gotten very far," said Kramer. "I didn't hear a car drive off."

"Let's go look," said Erv.

The two men ran around the building until they were directly behind the room that Marlowe was in. They stopped and scanned the darkness. There was little to see and the area was quiet. Suddenly a window next to Marlowe's room opened and a woman leaned her head outside.

"Are you guys looking for the guy who was next door?" she asked.

"Yes," said Erv. "Did you see where he went?"

"What are you guys...cops?"

"As a matter of fact," said Erv. "That guy is wanted for murder."

The woman pointed her finger into the dark woods. "Well, he actually fell when he crawled out the window but he got to his feet and took off over there into those woods."

The two men turned and stared into the darkness.

"Thank you so much," said Erv.

"Do you want me to call the police here in town?" she asked.

"No, thanks," said Erv. "We'll get him but thank you for your help."

Kramer turned to Erv. "Do you really think we can find him out there?"

Erv stared into the dark woods. "We got to try. Let's go."

The two men walked slowly across a small parking lot and then entered the dark woods. There was just enough light for them to see the outline of the massive trees. In such a case, they could easily grasp the tree and find their way around it. However, not every tree was easy to see, and that would result in one of the men walking straight into it.

"This could turn into a nightmare," said Kramer.

"How so?"

"It really looks like the old saying. We are looking for a needle in a haystack."

Erv froze and pointed a finger. "I just saw something moving."

"Was it Marlowe?" Kramer asked with a quiet voice.

"I'm not sure, but let's head in that direction just in case."

The two men walked softly as they approached a small clearing. They stopped and stood there in silence. It was a windless evening, and any sound could be heard for a very long distance. They stood there in silence for several minutes, and then it happened. They could hear the sounds of someone or something running away from them.

"What the hell was that?" Kramer asked.

"I couldn't tell if it was a man or an animal," said Erv. "But we need to keep going until we find out."

They started out again this time a bit faster in spite of the noise they created. Whatever or whomever they were pursuing seemed to be running at full speed in spite of the darkness and trees. Being a bit more cautious, Erv and Kramer ran much slower trying to avoid any unforeseen encounters with the trees or with the killer whom they were chasing.

Suddenly Erv slowed until he came to a complete stop. Kramer did as well.

"What's wrong?" Kramer asked.

Erv motioned for his brother to be quiet. They froze listening for any sounds that would direct them onto the right path. Nearly a minute passed and they heard nothing. They looked at each other and without speaking a word continued on trying effortlessly to avoid making any noises.

As they crept slowly through the darkened woods, whoever was leading would search for trees that might be in their path by waving his hands back-and-forth. Occasionally, he would slap one and the two men would make a quick bypass around it. The only thing that kept them going was the distant sounds of someone or something running away from them.

"Hold it," said Erv as he grabbed Kramer by the shoulder.

"What's the matter?" Kramer asked.

"We're not making any headway."

"So, what do you want to do?"

Erv pointed to the right of where they were going. "He seems to be traveling in an arc. He's probably fumbling around in the dark like us. If we were to cut across this way, we might be able to catch up with him."

"What do you think is going to happen when we come face-to-face with this guy?" Kramer asked. "He's already killed a dozen people. I don't think he's going to give up that easily."

"I have no idea," said Erv. "All I know is we will have to be very cautious. If he even looks like he's going for his gun, we will need to shoot him. We can't take any chances with this guy."

Suddenly a shot rang out. The two men dropped to their knees.

"Do you suppose he saw us?" Kramer asked.

"I don't know," said Erv. "He must have seen us. Why else would he fire a shot?"

"I think he fired a shot into the air to scare us and do what we're doing right now," said Kramer. "I'll bet he's off and running while we're sitting here."

Erv smiled. "I gotta hand it to ya. That's good thinking."

Kramer got to his feet. "Well, let's go find the bastard."

For the next several minutes they were able to slowly jog through the woods. It was obvious that they had run into a small clearing since neither one of them could see any trees in front of them. As they entered another section of the woods, they slowed their pace until they were walking slowly to avoid the trees.

"I wonder where he's at," said Kramer.

"I have no idea," said Erv. "Have you heard anything that would sound like him running?"

"Not a thing."

"Let's stop for a bit and see if we can hear anything."

The two men stood motionless for several minutes. They glanced at each other and scanned the area hoping to see something moving.

Then something happened. They both could hear the sound of something slashing in water and it was happening near them. The slashing soon stopped, and then came the sound of leaves rustling as if someone or something was running towards them.

"What the hell is that?" Kramer asked.

"I have no idea," said Erv as he pulled a flashlight from his pocket.

"I thought you said that shining that flashlight might be dangerous," said Kramer.

Erv turned it on and pointed it in the direction of the noise. After scanning the area, he finally centered the light on a pair of eyes that were glaring back at them.

"What the hell is that?" Kramer asked.

Erv paused as he scanned the body of the animal with the flashlight.

"Oh, my God!" said Kramer. "It's an alligator, and he's heading right for us!"

"Grab one of these skinnier trees and pull yourself up and out of his reach," said Erv.

Both men reached up and grabbed a branch and were able to pull themselves up far enough that the alligator was unable to reach them.

"Why didn't you shoot the bastard?" Kramer asked.

"Didn't have time," said Erv. "If I had missed he would have gotten one of us, and to me a fifty-fifty chance is not good enough."

"What do we do now?" Kramer asked.

"Well, the only thing we can do is shoot him," said Erv. "It doesn't look like he's leaving until one of us is his dinner."

Erv pulled out his gun and pointed it down at the animal. Just as he was about to pull the trigger, it turned and walked slowly away. Erv looked over at Kramer in disbelief.

"Did you see that?" Erv asked. "It was almost as if he knew what was coming."

"What are we going to do now?" Kramer asked. "There's no telling where he is now. We don't even know which direction he might have taken."

"I've got an idea," said Erv as he began to ease himself down to the ground. "Marlowe left just about everything he owns back there in that motel room. My guess he's heading back there to get his stuff. If we can move fast we might be waiting on him."

"Well, let's go," said Kramer.

With a flashlight pointing the way, the two men hurried through the woods. They were soon out of the densely populated woods and onto a clear pasture. In a short time they were back in Marlowe's motel room. They scanned the room and felt confident that he had not returned.

"Well, I would bet money that he will come back here to get his stuff," said Erv. "My guess this is everything that he owns."

Kramer scanned the room. "Ain't much, but I'll bet you're right. I'll bet he thinks we are lost out there in the woods and is set on coming back here to pick up his stuff."

"Well, we'd better get ready for him," said Erv. "He's going to be in a hurry to grab this stuff and get out of here."

"What should we do?"

Erv searched the room. "You go over there and hide behind that cabinet, and I will go over on that side of the room. We need to face him from two different angles. That way, he will know that he can't shoot both of us."

Kramer stared wide-eyed. "Well, what if he decides to take out one of us?"

Erv smiled. "I would suggest that you hide as much of your body as you can behind that cabinet and hope he is a poor shot."

Kramer smiled. "I guess when you think about it we are pretty safe. All he knows is how to stick his gun in somebody's ear. I can't imagine him shooting someone far away."

"Let's get set where we belong and wait for the bastard," said Erv.

The two men positioned themselves and sat back to rest. It was late at night, and both of these two men should have been exhausted. However, with the possibility of finally capturing this insane killer, they were both a bit nervous and very much excited.

"I can't believe that we might finally catch this guy," said Kramer. "This has been like a nightmare."

"I'll give you that one," said Erv. "I have never gone through anything like this."

"Do you think he has some mental issue?" "I guess to put it bluntly; do you think he's crazy?"

"Nobody with a normal brain kills that many people," said Erv. "He's got something seriously wrong with him. The sad thing is that if a head doctor declares him to be insane, he might possibly just get locked up for a few years, and we the taxpayers will pay for some doctor to straighten him out."

"He needs to be put to death," Kramer said. "And don't wait ten to twenty years to do it."

"It does make you wonder why this guy did this," said Erv. "What kind of a childhood did he have? Was he raised by normal people or did he have to take care of himself? That seems to be the normal way of things these days. Both parents are working and they hire someone to raise their kids."

"To tell you the truth I could care less about all of that," said Kramer. "What I'm concerned about is what he's going to do when he walks in this room. Is he going to shoot at us, and who's going to get it first?"

"If he's got any brains at all he will give himself up," said Erv. "We've got him in crossfire. He knows one of us will shoot him. He can't be that stupid."

Suddenly, Erv stared blankly at the wall. He motioned to Kramer to be quiet. "I hear something. Get ready."

The two men stared with wide eyes at the door as it slowly opened. It was Marlowe, and he was carrying a pistol in one of his hands. He slowly stepped inside cautiously pointing the gun in different directions.

"Hold it right there, Marlowe," said Erv. Marlowe turned and pointed the gun at Erv. "Don't even think about it. There are two of us, and the other one has a gun pointed at your back."

"Who are you?" Marlowe asked.

"I'm a cop," said Erv. "Now drop that gun."

Marlowe froze.

"Drop that God damn gun or I will put a hole in your head like you did to so many others."

Marlowe still did not move.

Kramer pulled back the hammer on his gun. The sound of it was heard by all.

Finally, Marlowe lowered his gun and dropped in onto the floor. Still cautious, Erv walked slowly over to the gun and kicked it over to Kramer who immediately bent over and picked it up.

"How long have you guys been after me?" Marlowe asked.

"Ever since you killed that woman in Cincinnati," said Erv.

"Relative?"

"She was our sister."

"Oh well...shit happens," said Marlowe with a slight grin.

"You raped her too, didn't you?" Erv asked with an angry voice.

"I sure did," said Marlowe. "But that was a mistake because she wasn't all that good anyhow."

Kramer lifted his gun and pointed it at Marlowe's head. He then began to slowly walk closer to him.

"No, Kramer," said Erv. "The asshole wants you to shoot him. Don't do it. He's a piece of shit and isn't even worth the bullet to kill him. You'll get in trouble, and he ain't worth it."

There was a long pause then Kramer finally lowered his gun and stepped back. "That's a first."

"What's that?" Erv asked.

"I've never wanted to kill someone that much," said Kramer. He then pointed at Marlowe. If you make one shitty move, I will shoot you in a heartbeat. Do you understand?"

Marlowe said nothing.

"Hey, dumbass, I asked you a question. Do you understand?"

"Yeah, yeah."

"Well, let's get his ass over to the sheriff's office," said Erv.

"I hate to ask you this, but do you have any handcuffs on you?" Kramer asked.

Erv paused. "No, I don't. I will drive and you can sit next to this guy in the backseat. Hopefully, he will do something, and you can put one in his ear."

Kramer smiled. "Let's go."

Thirteen

Dale Marlowe was finally locked up in a jail cell. His security was at the utmost and to prevent any wrong doing, a guard was assigned to watch over him. It had only been two days since his capture when his assigned lawyer arrived to introduce herself and to learn more about him.

"Hi, Mr. Marlowe, my name is Rachel Peterson. I will be representing you when your trial comes up," she said as she sat down.

"Jesus Christ! They're having a female represent me? What the hell is that all about?"

"Have you got a problem with that?" she asked.

"How many court trials have you done?"

"Does that matter to you?"

"Yeah, it sure does. I want someone with experience. Someone who can get me out of here." said Marlowe.

"Let's see. You admit to killing twelve people, and you think you might have a chance of getting out of here if you have a man representing you," said Rachel. "You're a special kind of stupid aren't you?"

Marlowe's face turned to anger. "You better be thankful that I'm wearing handcuffs."

"Mr. Marlowe, I don't want to be here anymore than you want me to be here. My goal is to do the best I can in your defense, and for me to do that I will need much information from you."

Marlowe leaned back. "Why even bother. We both know that I'm going to get the electric chair. Why waste your time?"

There was a pause as Rachel stared at Marlowe.

"Mr. Marlowe..."

"Call me Dale. There are no formalities here."

"With that being said, you can call me Rachel."

"We're practically best friends," said Marlowe. "Or even better yet we're practically lovers."

"That's not funny," said Rachel. "We're not here for fun and games. We are trying to keep you from being electrocuted. Do you have idea what that even looks like? Parts of your body will have smoke trickling off of them from the heat thrusts into your body. If you're really lucky, you will die immediately, but that doesn't happen every time. In fact, most of the executions take a minute or two for the person to die, so you get to sit there while two thousand volts of electricity flow through your body. Dale, have you ever had an electrical shock before from a light socket or a loose electrical wire?"

"Yes, I have," said Marlowe with a sober look on his face.

"That was a hundred and ten volts. Imagine two thousand!"

Marlowe paused. "Have you ever witnessed an execution?"

"Yes...yes I have, and I hope I never have to experience that again. I can't even imagine the pain. Can you imagine the shock being so great that your eyeballs pop out of your head? That happens. So, how 'bout you and me getting to work?"

Marlowe cleared his throat and sat straight in his chair. "Okay, you've got my attention."

"Just remember one thing," said Rachel. "Anything that you tell me is between you and me. It is private conversations, and nobody can force me to reveal what you have said to me. There is a law that prohibits anyone from trying to force me to tell them something that you told me. Do you understand?"

"So, anything I tell you is safe with you?" Marlowe asked.

"That's correct. Even if you tell me that you killed twelve people, I cannot be forced to reveal that."

Marlowe said nothing.

"Well..."

"Well what?"

"Did you kill twelve people?"

"Do you really want to know?"

Rachel paused. "Not really. Let's move on."

"Wait just a minute," said Marlowe. "You deserve to know the truth since you're going to be defending me. Yes, I did kill a mess of people. I don't know how many there were. I wasn't keeping track."

"Okay...Dale. Now I have a very important question for you. Do you have any idea why you did this? From what I can see you only knew that family of three in Ohio. Is that right?"

"Yeah, they were the only ones I knew," said Marlowe. "Why? Does it make a difference whether I knew them or not?"

Rachel paused then leaned back in her chair. "If you had just killed your in-laws, we might have got you a life sentence.

I could have presented things to the jury that would convince them that the family was asking for it, but that's out the window since you killed nine more people and you didn't even know them. That's telling the jury that you are crazy and the best thing for them to do is to have you executed."

"So what you're saying is that I don't have a chance," said Marlowe.

"Oh, yes, you have a chance, but it's a slim one," Rachel said. "What I'm going to do is get a psychologist to interview you and hopefully determine that you are sick and need help."

"I'm not sick," said Marlowe.

"Well, there are those who would think you are," said Rachel.

I can't help but think that I'm a normal person."

"Are you serious?"

"Just because I killed a few people doesn't make me sick in the head."

"You killed twelve people!" she shouted. "And you think that is normal?"

"I killed twelve people? I didn't realize that I had..."

"Obviously, you have something going on up there in your head that isn't right," said Rachel. "The only way we can keep you from being executed is to convince a head doctor and the jury that you are nuts. Otherwise, you are going to take a seat in an electric chair. Do you understand?"

"So what do you want me to do?" Marlowe asked.

"The first thing that will happen is you going in front of the judge. He will ask you how you want to plea. Are you pleading guilty or not guilty? This is simply court procedure. Nearly everyone pleads not guilty. Then he will tell us when the trial will happen. Hopefully, it will be months away so that we can get you in front of a head doctor. Understand?"

"Yeah... I gotcha."

"How was your childhood?" Rachel asked.

"What do you mean?"

"Was it a normal family with a mother and a father?"

"No...not really."

"Let me guess. Your father left before you were born, and your mother worked at a full time job."

"How did you know?"

"That's the story I hear from most all people who have committed a crime," said Rachel. "I think it's a problem here in the United States, and it's only going to get worse."

"That's funny," said Marlowe. "I thought it was the perfect childhood. I could go anywhere I wanted to and do just about anything and I didn't get into any trouble."

"That's the point I'm trying to make," said Rachel. "When you did something wrong there was nobody around to smack you and tell you that you had done something wrong. You do not learn right from wrong if you are not punished when you do something that you shouldn't have. That's what's going on in our country. There are those who grow up thinking that they can do anything they want. They think that it is their right to do unlawful things. Does any of this mean anything to you?"

"Oh, I'm sure that it should mean something, but I guess I just don't give a damn."

"You killed twelve people, and you don't care?"

Marlowe paused and then smiled. "If I had my way about it, everyone I encountered I would leave 'em dead."

Rachel stared blankly at Marlowe for a brief few seconds and then got to her feet.

"That's it. I can't take anymore of this," she said heading for the door. "I've got some work to do and will see you later."

The next day, Dale Marlowe was ushered into court by a policeman for his routine arraignment. He was there for only five minutes before the judge entered the courtroom. He asked that Marlowe and his lawyer approach the bench. After asking them whether they were pleading guilty or not guilty, Rachel replied, "Not guilty." The judge then set a trial date and then informed them that because of the seriousness of the crimes committed by Marlowe there would be no possibility of his release through bail money. Marlowe would have to remain in jail until his trial.

The days drifted by slowly. In the beginning, Marlowe was happy being locked inside the jail. He had a place to sleep, three meals each day and absolutely nobody bothering him. He was happy with this life style for the first month but then that certain happiness began to disappear. Boredom set in and soon took over his life. He became so anxious to see someone and talk to them that the arrival of the guard with his meal actually excited him. He tried desperately to entice the guard to talk with him but to no avail.

Six weeks had passed before the arrival of a psychologist. Bill Collins was a middle-aged man who was highly known for his expertise and accurate assessments of his clients. He was much too busy to take on another client, but when he was told who this man was, he put everyone else aside.

A guard led Collins to Marlowe's jail cell. He then sat down on a bench near the cell as a protective measure.

"Mr. Marlowe, my name is Bill Collins," he said extending his hand through the bars.

Marlowe got to his feet and shook his hand. "Nice to meet you."

"Let's skip the formalities," said Collins. "How 'bout first names?"

"Sounds good to me," said Marlowe.

"So, tell me, Dale, how's it going in here?"

"Oh, I guess it's alright. I was kinda glad when I first got in here. I'm not much of a people person. In fact, I prefer to be alone, and that's what you get in here. But after this many weeks of being alone and having nobody to talk to, I actually got a bit lonely. I am even thrilled when the guard brings me a meal. I never thought I would see the day."

"Do you deserve to be in here?" asked Collins.

"What do you mean?"

"Do you belong in jail for killing a certain amount of people, or are you an innocent person? Don't forget that whatever you say is between you and me."

Marlowe turned to see the guard who was by now sound asleep.

"Don't worry about him," said Collins. "Even if he was awake he couldn't hear us. I've known him for years, and he really can't hear a thing."

Marlowe smiled. "Oh, I belong in here. There's no question of that."

"How many people did you kill?"

"Oh, I don't know. I lost track. I think it was more than ten."

"It was an even dozen," said Collins. "You shot most of them in the ear. Why was that?"

"I don't know. Maybe so they couldn't hear anything I had to say," said Marlowe with a sheepish smile.

"No, no, I want you to tell me why you did that."

The smile on Marlowe's face disappeared. "I guess you didn't see the humor in that."

"Do you find humor in shooting a piece of metal into someone's head that tears a hole though the skin, through the skull and then through the brain? Some people might be lucky enough depending on the direction of the bullet that they might only lose their sight, their memory, their ability to function in society. Most of them, and I should refer to them as the luckier ones, die immediately. Actually, you do them somewhat of a favor by shooting them in the brain. Nearly everyone who is shot in the brain does not suffer for even a second. They are instantly dead."

Marlowe had a stern if not irate look on his face. "So what else do you want to talk about?"

"Did you ever go to one of the funerals that your actions created?" Collins asked with a sober face.

"No...not really."

"So you didn't see a mother kissing the coffin while they lowered it into the grave. You didn't watch as a child said good bye to a father or a mother as they turned and walked away from the gravesite. Makes you wonder, doesn't it?"

"Wonder about what?"

"Makes you wonder about a father or a son reading the newspaper about you and how angry they must be and how much they would love to kill you. It wasn't just about the people that you killed, it's also about the survivors. Some will never spend a day for the rest of their lives without remembering that loved one. How does that make you feel?"

"Oh, I suppose I'm sorry about it."

"You suppose? What if someone killed your mother and father? How would you feel about that?" Collins asked with a slight feeling of anger.

"I'd be thrilled to death," said Marlowe with a solid voice and a look of anger.

Collins sat up straight and leaned forward. "So, you'd be thrilled to death. Why do you say that? You must agree that such a statement is very strange. Normally, people find it very painful to lose a parent, and you say that you would be thrilled to death. Do you mind explaining that? What was your father like?"

"How the hell would I know? He left when I was a little kid. I hardly remember the asshole."

"So just about everything you learned was from your mother?"

"You're asking me if my mother taught me anything? Not really. She had a job, and I only had to put up with her a day or two each week and trust me that was more than enough."

"You sound as if your mother had problems," said Collins.

"Oh, she had problems," said Marlowe.

"Did you learn anything from her?"

"Yeah, I learned to stay away from her."

"Why do you say that?"

"Because she was mean to me."

"Did she spank you?"

"Every chance she could get."

"What else did she do to you?"

Marlowe bowed his head and stared at the floor. "I don't want to talk about it."

Collins leaned forward. "Dale, this is very important. I can tell something is wrong. What did your mother do to you when she disciplined you?"

"I don't think it's any of your business," said Marlowe with a stern voice.

"I want to make it my business because I think..."

Marlowe jumped to his feet. "She would drag me by holding onto my ear! We would be walking along and if I said something that she didn't like, she would grab my ear and drag me until blood was flowing out of it! Are you happy now?"

Collins paused with a saddened look. "I'm sorry, Mr. Marlowe. Did it affect your hearing?"

"Hell, yes, it affected my hearing," said Marlowe as sat back down.

"Did she do this more than once?"

"Are you kidding? She did it a million times!"

"Did you ever think that she was just trying to teach you right from wrong?" Collins asked. "There are many kids today that are not taught such..."

"Good God, man! This wasn't discipline. This was cruelty plain and simple."

Collins paused while he shuffled through papers. "All of the information given to me indicates that you shot nearly all of your victims in the ear. Is that true?"

"Well...yeah...I guess so."

"What do you mean by I guess so? You're the one who pulled the trigger. Right?"

"Yeah, okay. I shot every one of those bastards in the ear."

"Doesn't it seem like a coincidence that your mother pulled and consequently damaged your ear, and you shot a dozen people in the ear?"

Marlowe's face sobered. "What do you mean?"

"I mean that's quite a coincidence. Your mother was hurting your ear and you were shooting people in the ear. Was this your way of paying her back?"

Marlowe said nothing. He turned away and stared at the floor.

Collins got to his feet. "I have to go, but I will be back to discuss this a bit further. You think about what we were talking about. See you later."

It was several months later that the trial for Dale Marlowe began. Since the trial was in Florida, Marlowe was only being tried for the murder of the three hitchhikers in spite of the fact that he killed twelve people. It was to be an open and shut case. Even though Marlowe pleaded not guilty, there was more than enough proof for his conviction. As the trial progressed, it became abundantly clear that he was guilty. The only chance that he had to avoid the death penalty was for his lawyer to prove to the jury that he was mentally disturbed, but with all of the shocking evidence presented by the prosecutor there was very little chance for his survival.

As the trial got closer to the end, Collins decided to try one last desperate move. He decided that Marlowe should get on the stand. There were many who regarded such a procedure as a mistake since it allows the prosecutor the opportunity to ask questions that can be very detrimental. However, in Marlowe's case, it was already obvious that he was guilty and the only chance he had to survive an electrocution was to show a mental disorder. Collins had hoped that the testimony of the psychologist would reveal such a condition, but his testimony was not even close to being conclusive.

Marlowe was called to the stand. He took the oath to tell the truth and was seated in the witness chair.

Collins slowly walked up and stopped in front of Marlowe. "Now, Mr. Marlowe, how are you doing?"

Marlowe was wide-eyed with surprise. "Okay, I guess."

"Are they treating you okay?"

"Yeah...no problem."

"Well, that's good, Mr. Marlowe. That's really good," said Collins with a smile. "So tell me, Mr. Marlowe, what was your childhood like?"

"What d'ya mean?"

"Well, did you have a good father?"

"I don't know. I never really knew him."

"What do you mean you never knew him?"

"He got my ma pregnant and a few years later took off," said Marlowe. "That was too bad, 'cause I would have loved to have kicked his ass."

"So, the only parent you ever knew was your mother. How did she treat you?"

Marlowe paused and looked away.

"Mr. Marlowe I asked you a question. How did your mother treat you?"

"Not good," he said with a soft voice.

"Not good? Why do you say that?"

"Because she was mean to me."

"She was mean to you? What did she do that was mean?"

Marlowe began to rub his hands together. He turned and stared at a blank wall. "I don't know why, but she never did like me. Since she didn't have a husband, she had to work full time. I really didn't see her that much but when I did she was extremely mean to me. In fact, I can't remember anytime that she nice to me. I remember all of the Christmases we had when I was a little kid. The other kids in school would tell everyone what they got for Christmas. When they would ask me what I got I would have to lie because I never got anything. We didn't even have a Christmas tree."

"Did she ever hurt you?" Collins asked.

"Yes."

"What did she do?"

"She would beat me constantly, and I didn't even do anything wrong."

"What else did she do to you?"

Marlowe paused. "She would...she would grab my ear and pull me along while she was walking. She would continue doing it even though I was leaving a trail of blood behind us. Sometimes she would get so mad that I was leaving that blood that she would make me clean it off the sidewalk. I would rub and rub it, and it seemed to get even worse. She would then spank me for making it worse."

"How many times did she pull on your ear like that?" Collins asked.

"Oh, I have no idea. It's hard to remember a time when she didn't."

"That must have had a bad effect on that ear."

"Yeah, you can say that. I can't hear out of it."

"So you cannot hear out of one of your ears because of your mother's abuse. Is that correct?"

"That would be correct."

"Now Mr. Marlowe, isn't it a fact, that you shot most of your victims in the ear?"

"I guess so."

"Did you ever wonder why you did such a thing?"

"Not really."

"Well, it would seem to me that you were paying back your mother for what she did to you," said Collins.

"Objection, your honor," said the prosecutor getting to his feet. "Mr. Collins is not a licensed psychiatrist."

"Objection sustained," said the judge.

Collins turned back to Marlowe. "So, in spite of how your mother treated you, did you love her?"

"No...not really."

"Did you hate your mother?" Collins asked with a stern voice.

"Yes...yes I did."

"That seems a bit strange. Most people love their mother in spite of what she does."

"Most mothers don't treat their kids the way mine did."

"So tell me something, Mr. Marlowe," said Collins his voice growing louder. "You shot most of your victims in the ear. Do you think that has anything to do with your mother destroying your ear?"

"Objection, your honor," said the prosecutor. "The defense is asking for an opinion not facts."

The judge hesitated then said, "Over ruled. Let's listen to what Mr. Marlowe has to say."

Everyone in the courtroom went silent. All eyes turned to Marlowe.

"Do you need me to repeat the question?" Collins asked.

"No, not really. I guess I never put two and two together. I never really thought about such a thing, but now when I think about it, I was probably paying back my mother for what she did."

"Your witness," said Collins as he returned to his seat.

The prosecutor in this case was Mr. Matt Murdza. He was a considerably young man at the age of forty but had established a reputation of being the most successful prosecutor of all times. He walked across the courtroom and stopped in front of the seated Marlowe. He leaned over with his face just inches from Marlowe's face.

"Okay, Mr. Marlowe, let's skip all the rhetoric and foolishness, and I don't care about how many you killed here in Florida. Just answer one question for me. Did you kill twelve people?"

Marlowe said nothing. He turned to the judge and then to his lawyer.

"Well?" Murdza asked. "I don't care where you shot them or any of that junk. Did you kill twelve people? I need a simple yes or no."

Marlowe looked down at the floor and then back at Murdza. "Yeah...I killed them...all twelve of them."

Dale Marlowe was found guilty for killing the three Florida residents and was sentenced to be electrocuted in the electric chair. Over the years there were many court appeals, but to no avail. Dale Marlowe was to be strapped in the electric chair and put to death.

Eleven years after his conviction, Dale Marlowe was moved to another building that was called death row.

It was April 21, 1993, the day proclaimed by a jury of twelve people to be the last day on earth for Dale Marlowe. The morning dawned with warm sunshine as spring was in the air.

A key rattled in a steel door, and a guard carrying a tray of food entered. Marlowe was sitting on the edge of his bed with his head in his hands.

"Good morning, Mr. Marlowe," said the guard sliding the tray into the cell.

"Morning, Mr. Miller," Marlowe muttered.

"Get any sleep?"

"Not a wink."

"That's good."

"Why do you say that?"

"Dulls the senses," said Miller. "You're less aware of what's going on."

Marlowe glanced at the tray. "I don't think I can eat a bite. I'll just throw it back up."

"Well, I'll just leave it there just in case you get hungry."

Marlowe sat up and turned to the guard. "What's it like. Mr. Miller?"

"What's what like?"

"You know..."

"Oh, I don't want to talk about it."

"It's okay, Mr. Miller. Just tell me what you know."

"Well, I don't know much about what goes on. All I know is that they'll come to get you sometime late this afternoon shortly after you have your last meal. They're going to take you over to a little building called the death house. What goes on in there, I can only guess."

"Surely you must have heard."

"Not interested. No, siree. Never even been inside that place."

"I take it you don't believe in the death penalty."

"No opinion, one way or the other. I just don't want any part of the execution of a man."

Marlowe put his head in his hands. "I tell you it's got me so scared I'm pissing my pants." He looked up at Miller. "I got to know. Is it fast and painless?"

"You don't want to know."

"So you do know what happens. Somebody told you, didn't they?"

"Let's just say it's over with in less than ten minutes."

"Ten minutes! You mean to tell me I'm going to burn in that thing for ten minutes. How many volts do they use?"

"I don't know."

"Yes, you do. Now tell me how many?"

"Someone said that it's 2,000 volts."

"They're going to pass 2,000 volts through my body, and it will take ten minutes to kill me! Oh, good Lord help me. Think of the pain that I will have to endure."

"Actually, I heard there is no pain involved. The first jolt knocks you out. You don't feel a thing."

Marlowe slowly shook his head. "I'd like to believe that. Besides, how would anybody know?"

"Sorry, Mr. Marlowe," said Miller and slowly walked out of the room.

It was a little after four in the afternoon when he ate his last meal. As was the tradition, he was allowed to have anything he wanted. He had fried oysters, fried chicken, chili con carne, potatoes, limburger cheese spread, bread, butter, coffee, grape juice, orange juice, vanilla ice cream with chocolate syrup, and chocolate cake.

He originally extended an invitation to reporters to come and watch him eat his last meal but declined to see newsmen during his final day of life. When he finished his meal, he was taken back to his cell on death row to await the trip to the death chamber.

Marlowe collapsed on the edge of his bed. His legs shook so badly he could hardly stand. His hands quivered as if he were having convulsions. He leaned back on the bed and fell asleep.

At 5:45, two guards entered his cell and helped him get to his feet. They shackled his hands and feet and led him out of the room. They escorted him down hallways and through locked doors until they were outside in the cool April air. It was a short walk to the death chamber, but Marlowe shivered, convulsively, all the way.

As they reached the door to the death chamber, Marlowe's legs buckled. One of the guards reached out and helped him to walk the last few feet. At 6:00, they locked him in the death cell. The time for his execution had been set for 8:00. Dale Marlowe had only two hours to live.

An hour later, the door opened. Marlowe jumped. It was Father Lucier, the penitentiary Catholic chaplain. He sat next to Marlowe and began to slowly read from the Bible. By then, Marlowe was dazed and didn't hear a word he muttered.

At 7:55, Warden Alvis, three physicians, the executioner, and 17 witnesses filed into a small room. They crowded around the walls facing a wooden chair perched on a small platform. The warden tapped twice on a door. The door opened, and the priest slowly walked into the room softly reciting the Lord's Prayer over and over. Then Marlowe appeared, his eyes closed and his head bowed. He was praying aloud with the priest. The two guards supported him as he walked to the chair.

With some degree of effort, Marlowe stepped upon the platform, and with help from the guards eased into the chair. By then, his mutterings of the Lord's Prayer were indiscernible, punctuated with quiet sobs.

Marlowe grew silent as two guards began to strap him in. Straps were fastened around his wrists, his forearms and ankles. As they positioned his legs into the metal clamps, one of the guards dipped a rag into a bucket of saltwater and soaked the clamp and leg area. The other guard then tightened the clamp firmly around his legs.

One of the guards once again dipped the rag into the brine and swabbed the electrodes. Marlowe flinched as he attached them to his head. The guard paused and then leaned over to whisper into Marlowe's ear. He stood erect, then lowered a black mask over his head. He and the other guard and Father Lucier stepped back from the chair. Marlowe dug his fingernails into the handles of the chair. Silence filled the room as all eyes turned to the warden. Some of the witnesses quietly wept, while others turned away.

The warden nodded to the executioner. He reached to the wall and pulled a large handle. A blue light that was on the wall behind Marlowe went off, and a red one flashed on.

Marlowe's body lurched upward tearing at the straps. His body remained rigid, the tendons and veins of his neck and legs standing out against the reddening flesh.

Father Lucier finished the Lord's Prayer alone.

As the powerful current passed through his body, his fists remained clenched and resting on the arms of the chair. The hum of the generator became quiet, and the red light was replaced by the blue one. His body slumped deep into the chair. Fifteen seconds had passed. Many of the witnesses who had looked away, now slowly and cautiously turned back to the macabre scene.

After the passage of another fifteen seconds, the blue light gave way to the red, and Marlowe's body again lunged against the confining straps. The powerful jolt of electricity crackled and snapped as it seared through his body. Faint wisps of smoke rose from the electrode around his leg swirling between his knees and seeped through the cotton mask that covered his head.

As the lights again changed, the reddened flesh about his chest and throat turned to a bluish-black color. His head was thrown back, and once again he slumped into the chair, this time motionless. The business of killing was silent now. The only sound was the quiet weeping of witnesses.

A prison doctor approached Marlowe. He carefully pulled back his shirt revealing his blackened chest. For two minutes, he probed with his stethoscope searching for any signs of life. He stepped aside, and another doctor made his examination. He turned to the spectators and said, "Sufficient electricity has passed through the body of Mr. Dale Marlowe to have caused death at 8:09 p.m."

The warden and the witnesses filed out of the room. Two guards removed the remains from the chair and took them to a waiting hearse. The body of Dale Marlowe was buried in the ground at the end of the day on April 21, 1993.

⅄ ⅄ ⅄

Erv Meyers was sitting in his favorite easy chair when the front door opened. His brother Kramer Meyers stepped inside and closed the door. He stared at the mass of empty beer cans lying on the floor.

"Good God, Erv! You don't even throw your beer cans in the trash?"

"I will when I get up," said Erv.

"Do you mean that you drank this many since you sat down?"

"Actually I have gotten up a few times to pee, but I'm not done watching television. I'll get a shovel when it's time."

"Well, anyway, I have some news for you," said Kramer sitting down on a kitchen chair. "They finally executed Marlowe."

"They did? When did this happen?"

"Last night. He's finally underground where he belongs."

"Yeah...I guess so," said Erv with a saddened look on his face.

Kramer paused as he studied his brother. "You look depressed. What's wrong with you?"

"I'm sorry that he was executed."

"You're kidding me," said Kramer with a look of surprise. "He killed twelve people. Isn't that reason enough to fry his ass?"

"No...not really. He should be locked up for the rest of his life, but not killed."

"You don't believe in capital punishment, do you?"

"No, I don't," said Erv. "That's something for God to do. Not us."

"Well, this is a shocker to me. I had no idea you were the religious type," said Kramer.

"You can call it religious. I call it common sense."

"Well, I don't know whether you are ready for this or not, but there's another killer on the loose."

Erv leaned forward. "How many has he killed?"

"Three, so far."

Erv paused for a moment then got to his feet. "Well, then, let's go."

THE END

SCOTT FIELDS
THE AUTHOR

In 1966, Scott turned down a contract with the Detroit Tigers to pursue his lifelong dream of becoming a published author by earning a degree at Ohio University. In 1996 with a lifelong

dream of being a writer, Scott started writing short stories. Within two years, he had four stories published. Since then, his first novel, **All Those Years Ago**, was published, **Summer Heat**, his fifth novel, was published in May 2012 and his most recent, **The Mansfield Killings**, based on a true story, was published in October 2012. To date, Scott has published 15 novels.

Now, Scott spends nearly all his time writing his next novel.

Scott lives in Mansfield, Ohio, where most of his novels take place, with his wife, Deb.

Visit his web site, **www.scottcfields.com** to learn more.

www.ingramcontent.com/pod-product-compliance
Lightning Source LLC
Chambersburg PA
CBHW071346250626
47159CB00004B/1621